CUYAHOGA

A NOVEL

PETE BEATTY

SCRIBNER

New York London Toronto Sydney New Delhi

Scribner
An Imprint of Simon & Schuster, Inc.
1230 Avenue of the Americas
New York, NY 10020

First Scribner hardcover edition October 2020

SCRIBNER and design are registered trademarks of The Gale Group, Inc., used under license by Simon & Schuster, Inc., the publisher of this work.

For information about special discounts for bulk purchases, please contact Simon & Schuster Special Sales at 1-866-506-1949 or business@simonandschuster.com.

The Simon & Schuster Speakers Bureau can bring authors to your live event. For more information or to book an event, contact the Simon & Schuster Speakers Bureau at 1-866-248-3049 or visit our website at www.simonspeakers.com.

Illustrations by Adam Villacin

Manufactured in the United States of America

1   3   5   7   9   10   8   6   4   2

Library of Congress Cataloging-in-Publication Data is available.

ISBN 978-1-9821-5555-1
ISBN 978-1-9821-5557-5 (ebook)

For Anna

Stories will go to rot without puttingup. You must salt them into Egyptian mummies, or drown them in lying sugar. Bury them in winter and freeze their blood.

But you would hide the honest stink, the moschito bites, the wounds, the living glory.

Let you and me do without salt and sugar. Taste matters true – even if the truth is half rotten.

Winter.

A tidy house, under bedclothes of snow, every window dark. The night is empty. No moon, no dogs, no drunks. No night pigs wondering after food. Not even a hungry hoofprint.

The eye is the lamp of the body and yours shows on *The city of Ohio at the third hour of the year 1837.* A lamp is no use without more to look at. Go ahead and enter the house. I will watch for constables walking bundled against the cold. It is fine – we go as haints. Haints cannot be criminals.

Inside is no mansion but there are modest riches. You see a young mother abed, a cherub child tucked in a cradle at mother's feet, a house-cat the size of a hog, a family Bible, brass candlesticks, clean swept floors, quilts, stick furniture – nothing fancy but good for sitting. This feels a home. A respite on the long flight from Eden.

Your lamp beams brighter and soon you see the absences between comforts. No axe or man's britches hung by the door. Perhaps this is a widow's home. You think a widow must always be tragic. But look at the cheerful aspect of this place. Even the bedpots have a pleasant look.

As you haint around, the light of your lamp-eye keeps to growing. Such that it beams brighter than day, and the air breathes warmer, stifling even. The woman abed begins to stir. You turn nervous at being seen.

Crap. This is poor luck. Look behind you. We have started a *fire*. Flames is lapping up the wall. How has this— Did your burglar eyes spill their blaze? Have you done this? You set the domestic tenderness to burning. With your eye. I do not know how.

Douse it in blankets – hurry.

Not that one – that is too fine a quilt.

Have they got any water?

Get out of the damned house.

Back to the snow-shrouded lane. You are agitated and scorched. You are safe. But we have not done the courtesy of rousting the home. Through the cackle of flames come the cries of widow and beautiful child and plump cat. Even as the devil's laughter rolls and the wailing sharpens you hear a sudden *thwock*. It must be timbers snapping at the heat – or the family Bible ignited, shocked by the blaspheming fire. And another *thwock*.

As alarms spread to the neighbor houses you hear calls for buckets. Folks yell *FIRE* as if to shame the blaze, but it only cackles back. The widow is hollering for the Lord to take the household up quick, but only the *thwock* answers.

The fire has roused the whole town. We are no longer alone – the sounds of tragedy is joined by hoots of alarm and barking church bells. Every soul for a mile around is singing out for *Buckets buckets buckets. Thwock thwock thwock* the house says back.

Nothing draws folks out like a house in flames – soon enough there is chatter and snowball tossing mixed in with the *Buckets!* and widow's wails and *thwock*s. Do not think the neighbors unchristian. Some are still whiskey-drunk from greeting the New Year. *Thwock.* In the absence of a sing or a nut-gathering there is nothing like a house afire to stir us up. I do not propose the burning of widows and babes for sport. Only that a house afire is a credible substitute for the sun. Especially at winter. Preserves carry the ghost of summer. You yourself are transported some by the blaze – I can see so by your face.

Thwock.

Your clumsiness has set all this going. Folks seem to drop from trees to gawp. Boys fool, men mutter, women pray. *Thwock.* The call for buckets dies down and so do the wails from inside. There is only the rough breath of flame and the *thwock.* But even the *thwock* ceases.

Just as you are certain the house must fall – must make a grave of itself – the flaming front door bursts open. Out of the smoke steps the charred shape of a man. Stooped, staggering, he stumbles but does not fall. He carries with him the young widow. Does she still draw breath?

This roasted rescuer heaves the widow onto a snowbank

and falls to his knees. Steam rolls from his back and the winter white melts in a circle around him. A sooted arm goes into the breast of his blouse and comes out with the baby, who screams with wonder at being rescued. At this cry the mother awakens – she lives! Our hero reaches into his shirt again and produces the halfhog cat, its furs singed some. As the cat runs off – dignity busted into a thousand pieces – the angel of the fire breathes heavy. The crowd takes a reverent quiet.

You are a shambles to know who this man is. His shoulders wide as ox yokes. A waist trim as a sleek lake schooner. Muscles curlicued like rich man's furniture. Chestnut hair shining in the orange light of the blaze. A cheerful red cloth knotted at his neck. His small bright eyes look up and he drinks another great breath, which comes out as a laugh. A church organ full of the sacrament wine. And he says *Who has brought refreshment?*

Now you have met my brother Big Son.

In the stories you are used to, a stranger arrives at the castle, or the king is gnawed by crisis. Swords bang together. Ghosts trouble a pale hero. Lovers' hearts boiling. We drink down such wild stories to drown our worries. They are whiskey to wash out our brains.

My brother's stories are more apple cider. They are good to drink but you will not forget yourself entirely. Wholesome tales, without too many fricasseed widows. True mostly – I will not lie any more than is wanted for decency. Simple and moral, easy to grab, the better to encourage someone over the head with. Not too quiet – you must not fall asleep. Let us have commerce and racing horses. Progress and the mastery of nature. Swap swords for axes and plows. Let us have tenderness but also a dash of cussedness and tragedy. All in the manner native to Ohio.

In this story lovers' hearts do not boil but go slowly like stew. The crisis has got square cow's teeth instead of fangs. There is not a king to be seen. Only my brother as hero.

And we will have a stranger at the castle.

I will take that good part.

My name is Medium Son.

We are no longer strangers any – folks call me Meed.

My brother were democratic in his feats. He done them in a hundred different patterns like calico. Big – he is mostly called Big – rastled bears and every other creature ten at a time. Drank a barrel of whiskey and belched fire. Hung church bells one-handed. Hunted one hundred rabbits in a day. Ate a thousand pan cakes and asked for seconds. Drained swamps and cut roads et c. More feats than I have got numbers to count up.

I thrilled most at his brawling with the world itself. At his domesticating Lake Erie and several rivers besides. At his strength turned against soil and stone. There is nothing like the making of a place. To bust up creation. To write your name in the very earth. My brother was a professor of such work.

You have heard of Daniel Boone – Colonel Crockett – Mike Fink – other American Herculeses. My brother shown the same appetites.

You ask *Why is this Big Son not the hero of every child?* *What feats of his do I know?*

Do not burn houses every day. But when you do burn them look for my brother. You cannot keep him away from any fire greater than a lucifer match. There is a song inside burning wood and my brother hears it keener than anyone. This taste comes from his first feat nine years ago when he whipped ten thousand trees.

I imagine you are customed to meek and mild trees that do not want correcting. This is a story of the west so it has got western trees. You do not know the manners of our trees. I have told you that my brother and I dwell in the city of Ohio, which sits on the western bluff at the mouth of the Cuyahoga, looking across that crooked river at the city of Cleveland on the eastern bluff. Put this map in your mind.

In 1796 Connecticut surveyors come through and said that there ought to be a town called Cleveland. They did not bother any with making the town, only with drawing it on their maps. The first settlers found the place full of discouragements, such as moschitos, ague, and poorly behaved wildlife wanting chastisement.

A mule's character were evident in the population from the first. The settlers kept on past the discouraging and their infant town Cleveland had grown up to one thousand souls by the year 1828.

Your true mule westerner does not prefer one thousand neighbors. As Cleveland grown, handfuls of folks spilled across the river looking for an emptiness more to their liking. My brother and I – orphans in the care of Mr Job and Mrs Tabitha Stiles – went among these handfuls.

In order to make a good emptiness you have got to clear land. The trees on the western bluff, having seen the demise of their eastern kin, was wary. But we only nibbled out our few acres and kept a glass-thin peace with the woods.

The trouble come when the nibbling spread out into eating-up.

As winter of 1828 cleared out, the handfuls coming across the river become sackfuls, every man among them taking his bite out of the woods. The western trees – oaks and elms and plump sycamores by the dozen thousand – whispered by breezes as their buds came in. They said *We must get shut of these fleas.*

Soon folks found trees sprouting up where they had

just cleared ground. Plots vanished. Dead timber fell onto homesteads without any storm blowing them over. Firewood piles took to disappearing.

We fleas fought back. I were barely ten years and too young to swing an axe to any use but I remember spring air felt as warm as summer on account of all the chopping. Every man's axe has got a voice to it *nock   chsnk   gntk   dnnk*   A hundred different words saying the same meaning.

All the axe talk had romance in it but the trees was not enamored any. They only grew back faster and thicker than before. Thieved back plots already cleared. Branches were seen to bust into windows and doors and carry off animals and merchandise. Have you ever felt the breath of an angry tree? It has a cold carelessness.

After a week of this awful spring, a fear settled on us. A worry that we had found the limits of the republic. That we should stop at the eastern side of the Cuyahoga. That we had gotten to the bottom of the west. That the continent would revolt and fling us back into the ocean.

You have already heard the pure and pretty *thwock* of my brother's axefall as he cut his way into the widow's house. You ask why it were not heard among the choir. Is not the merest smell of Big Son enough to scare trees worse than one thousand beavers? At the year 1828 Big were not yet the hero you have met. His hair hardly shone. He had not yet learned to *thwock*.

When the half-child Big announced at the second Sun-

11

day of spring that he would clear the timber in two days and a night, the men fleas could only laugh. A mean type of laugh. They said they would like to see it. They said such comedy would lift their spirits. They said *Go ahead* and even borrowed my brother a good axe.

Before a jug could be fetched, my brother smashed into the trees, his borrowed blade curling back the edges of the air. Trees and fleas alike kept at laughter, but before any too long the comedy gone out. The timber saw that Big were no regular flea, and us regular fleas stared in wonder. Even my young eyes knew it right away. Even curious squirrels and birds and ground hogs known to stop and watch. All creation likes a miracle.

Big knocked down a dozen trees in the first quarter of an hour, before the forest took him serious. After that brave beginning, the match turned some. A long mean locust grabbed Big up in a branch and flung him deep into the wood – where the trees stood so close you could not see the doings. Only the sounds of Big gasping and *thwock*ing, leaves shaking, branches snapping. Here and there a flash of his blade or his hair catching the sideways afternoon sun. A tree top sinking down in defeat. A startled deer bolting.

Such commotion gone for hours on end. A rastle will make a crowd but it cannot keep one without enough pummeling. Boredom come on. The fleas drifted off to supper, the creatures went off to a more peaceful corner of the woods, and finally the sun itself made to wander off, tired of lighting an unwatched match. Only two spectators remained – myself and Mr Job Stiles.

You will meet Mr Job better in the course of matters, but let me draw him quick. He were spare and stretched out, made of knitting sticks. He wore a thin brown fringe of beard on his pointed chin and a preacherly straw hat tilted back on the crown of his head. He always spoke like he were sorry at the situation. In this case it were called for. The sounds of Big's fight gone down to a mutter and then nothing at all. Surely he had been pummeled to surrender. Mr Job said we ought to get home for dinner, and that I ought to fetch my brother.

I will not lie – I did not care to do what Mr Job asked. I were afraid of the dark and of creatures and of finding my brother busted past mending. But I trusted and still do trust in Mr Job. I known he would not put me to work I could not stand. There were enough of the sun dripping down through leaf and branch that I could see.

That light thinned as I made my way deep and deeper into the wood. After a half mile I got to a clear and saw the very last of the light glinting off something at the bottom of a great ironwood. An axe blade. As I come closer the spring air went out of my blood and the winter ice come back in. For the second time in my life – you will know the first later on – I were looking at my brother's dead self. The axe were tucked into his arms just like a burying Bible, with the last bit of dusk as a shroud.

Yet! As I inched toward him in despair I seen that the dusk did not shine in my brother's hair. I seen at close examine that this were not hair at all but a clutch of twigs arranged as a wig. His skin were not skin at all but birchbark. But these were surely the britches and blouse of my brother – he had been turned to wood – this were too much – this were witches.

Just as I ran a finger over the bark of his cheek, sleep came over me like I were thrust into a sack. I slumbered hot and itching. I dreamt that I seen my brother, alive and naked as a babe, moving in and out of the timber, the blue moonlight on his rear.

From the light I known it were the middle of morning. What I did not know was where I were. The air stunk of sawdust and smoke. My skin and clothes were painted all over with ashes. All around me was a town I did not know, with a wide-eyed look to everything. Like it were only just born. Houses and stores and barns, all naked yellow wood. What was this place? I met our neighbors and friends – Mr Dennes and Mr Philo and Mr Ozias – straggling through, smacked dumb. I were in the same way. I could only blink and turn my head around in wonder. I would still be there stumped except I heard another *MEED*. This time not a whisper but a lusty holler from beyond the new buildings. Before long a scorched and still-naked Big came out of the alien lanes, dragging his axe and a wild tale.

Meed, those trees wore me to tatters   I were tossed back and

14

forth for hours even as I cussed bad as I knew   All the time I
flew across the sky my brains kept kicking   At night's coming,
the trees tired of sport and set me down but left a sentry   A great
grandpa ironwood minded me while the forest went to its evening
chores He waved the axe toward the stump what marked the
ironwood. *And I made a pantomime that the scrap had put me to*
sleep   Soon through a cracked eye I seen that the ironwood was
abed too and—

I knew right then what he had done. I have always had
a head for understanding Big. His pride were spilling out
of him in nervous talk. Let me make you a present of the
trimmed and tidy account.

The trees gave my brother a thrashing and expected he
would sleep politely. This faith were their undoing. Once
Big saw his guard-tree were dozing he slipped from liar-
sleep and made a liar-self from sticks and bark. He left the
false Big into the arms of the ironwood, along with his axe
– the *thwock*ing of which would have woken up all the forest. Around this time I shown up and he panicked I would
spoil his sneaking – so he gently knocked me over the head
and laid me down next to his doll. All night he peeled and
scotched and girdled, gathered up kindling. Just before the
sun stirred from rest, he ran naked through the arbor and
lit one hundred fires.

The trees awoke to the dawn of their own burning, with
the true sun hid behind the blue smoke. They panicked to
find themselves trussed up by Big's night-work. My brother

did not make any deathbed sacraments for his rivals. Instead he grabbed up his axe from the hands of his false self and went wild with progress. He butchered the trees in a dozen ways. Pulling one up and swinging it as a club into another. Busting one over his knee. Sending one tumbling into its cousins like tenpins. Smiling as he went – leaving stumps and holes and busted tree-bones all over. His work were never tidy.

Dawn stirred into day and Big kept toward chewing up the whole western forest. Before too long the fleas was awake and watching – eyes following the shining hair even as the boy underneath looked more a man with every smasher. Finally he felt those flea eyes and ceased his work – huffed some – looked around at his mess – turned to the fleas – spread out his arms like an actor and said *Go ahead*

At first they moved with cautious wonder, sniffing and kicking at the jumbles of felled timber. But before long caution turned to greed and the fleas ran to claim up the best lots. They set straight to carpentry and knit the still-warm wood into homes and barns and stables and stores, all in a morning. And then I awoke and heard the story straight from Big – how Ohio city, the sister and rival of Cleveland, come to be.

The waters of the west was generally more polite than the trees. At first neither the Cuyahoga nor Lake Erie seemed cross at the slaughter of the forest. The river kept snoring away like a greenbrown sow, but a scowl stole into the lake. Every day we was washing up – fishing – emptying night pots – baptizing – tanning skins – soiling the waters.

Before too long the lake took to fussing at us. But we only acted worse for all the storms and shipwrecks. Sending steamboats crawling across the lake's face. Spreading ourselves wider and wider along the bluffs. Spilling more mess every day. Finally in the fall of 1829 the lake unleashed a wild wind, lasting for weeks on end. A good many trees spared by my brother keeled over. Fences and barns and houses fell. Churches was shorn of steeples. Children and other small livestock was carried away, never to be seen again. Soon we thought to rope tender creatures down, but both Cleveland and Ohio city spent that season in fear, near undone by the lake's fury.

Big Son did not see any sense in such tyrannical conduct. After some weeks of constant storms, he marched down to the water's edge, his hair flapping wet, and proceeded to scold about the inevitability of white folks – that this revolt was foolishness – plumb stupid – that the lake could *blow*

17

*and bite all you wanted but we are here for eternity and you ought
to go along like a fellow*

The lake did not talk back but its brownblue shade of
summer turned to greenblack, and you could see it were
drunk on its own might.

Big seen that scolding was not the remedy. He tried to
ambassador instead, saying *Come now Erie, let us be pals*   He
opened his arms out wide like he would embrace the mil-
lion acres of water.

Wouldn't you know the lake rose up and slapped him in
the chops with stinging waves. Big grinned as wide as creation and leapt in for a fight.

Man and water brawled for a fortnight. My brother first
went after Erie with his axe, but that did no good. You cannot
thwock water. Next he tried to drink up the whole lake. But his
guts rebelled after he had swallowed down six feet, though
Erie is still shallow for it – a token of Big's admiration.

In a fight, waters go for drowning every time. But Big
has the lungs of an elephant and could dunk for a day and
night without gasping. The fight gone on and on, such that
those who gathered to watch and wager took boredom. So
no one saw when the lake finally got Big by the shining hair
and tied him to a sunken schooner. Big kicked and fussed
awfully and pled for a Samaritan but a fish cannot untie a
knot. After some hours of this he finally spread his hands
and bubbled *UNCLE*

The lake were battered too, relieved to toss him to shore.
Lakes do not like to have a dead body in them any more

than a body likes to be dead. But this particular body should not have been trusted. Big were already at trickery even as he coughed up a perch and gobbled lungfuls of autumn air.

Mr Erie   I have got a bargain for you   We all will pack up our towns and head right back east in the morning   You just give me one good quiet night to rest   No wind, no rain, no bitter cold

The lake, sore from the rastle, took the bait.   *Alright, Mr Big Son   You have fought hard and you shown a considerable common sense   I will do what you ask*

So my brother and the lake they shook on it – climbed into their sleeping clothes and laid down to await the last day of Ohio city.

As soon as the lake bedded down, liar Big went digging for the greatest rock he could find. If the lake might pin him to a shipwreck, then surely he could pin the lake to the soil beneath. He would find a boulder so great that Erie would have no choice but to behave. He snuck to Handerson and Panderson's emporium and borrowed himself a good three-dollar shovel. He dug all through the night, but he only found regular-sized rocks. From his deep hole Big saw that dawn were crawling into the sky and Erie would soon awake. Around this moment, his shovel uncovered a great oaken door facing upward. Through the cracks Big marked a murmur of bloodred flame and the stink of dead folks within.

He suspected just whose roost this were and what would come of calling – but he took to reasoning. The father of lies surely knew where the largest rocks were on account of landlording deep within the earth. And Big were already a

19

liar for his false deal with the lake – the devil would appreciate such work. Big's dishonest heart would want washing out
on next Sunday already, so he might soil it further without
fear. So my brother whanged at Hell's door with his shovel.

There were some clattering inside and creaking floor-
boards but soon enough the door swung open. The host
what met him were not a scarlet-skinned demon dripping
with fiery snots, but a white man aged about fifty years –
unshaved and tired around the eyes – dressed in a blanket
and nightcap, but not cross at his caller. The devil seen Big
into his parlor and poured him good storebought coffee.

You think on Satan taking Christ to the mountain and
making his propositions. *Back me and I will make you master
of a dozen cities   Fix us bread to eat from these rocks   Jump off
the temple roof to show how much man you are*   These were
foolish baits that only a fool would bite. Since Bible times,
the Adversary had learned better lines of talk. If the devil
tricked my brother, he made it look like Big had the idea
first.

As they took their coffee, Big put down the bargain – if
he might have a suitably large rock from Lucifer, then he
could subdue the tyrant lake and ensure the future prosperity of the two towns of the Cuyahoga.

The devil did not ask what were in it for him, apart from
his general appetite for deceit. In fact he sounded like any
politician. *I back the United States all day long   I back progress
every time   I am for democracy   For whatever keeps you all busy
and growing*

Big were not sure what this meant, but he waited polite.

I only ask that I might have a few prime city lots as a security for my coming old age said Satan.

Big had no lots to give away and did not like to lie more. But is it a sin to lie to the devil?

By the time Big drug his great boulder up, the sun were risen. The lake were still dozing, even as early-to-work wagons clonked through muddy lanes and bacon nickered in pans. The lake were still dozing even as Big tugged the rock up to the Lakewood cliff – still dozing to the very moment the vast hell-hot stone thundered into its guts.

The lake tumbled out of sleep screaming about the tricks of Big Son but couldn't hardly roar with such a boulder in its belly. Ever since Erie does not misbehave too much – only frowns and dreams of someday drowning us.

Big's feats gone on in this general way for years – my brother proved himself a foremost spirit of the times. You are familiar with how a spirit of the times done. Tamed bears, rastled the pope of Rome, romanced queens and milkmaids. Half horse and half alligator and another half wolverine set on top. Et c. In truth Big did not meet the pope any and never seen any queens. It is only a manner of talking. Pope or no, my brother were red pepper at Sunday supper.

You know how red pepper tastes. Loud and foolish. My brother has got quieter flavors to him as well. Tenderness cussedness and tragedy as I promised. I will put these down directly.

But I must do a bit more mumbling before I put down the tales. I do not wish to *sell* you my brother. To recite him like news paper advertisements. To sweat over him like a tent preacher.

Though I do believe I could make a decent merchant for him as a foremost spirit of the times.

But he is not an article of merchandise.

Although when I grease my mind some, I consider a spirit *is* alike to an article of merchandise. If you will permit wider talk. Every age and place has got its Big Sons. Folks who hang the sky that we shelter under. Stand up the timbers of a place. Some of the timbers is timbers and others is more like ideas. The spirits of the time make a place more than Connecticut surveyors and maps.

There was Courthouse Shad of Painesville, who put law on the blizzards and bargained them into a treaty. They could snow the town to the waist four months a year so long as they behaved the rest.

In Conneaut it were Finland Pete, who dug a harbor with one belch.

In Newburgh you had Wagonface – a fascination whose face were wider than tall. He had ears round as wheels. I cannot remember what feats Wagonface done but I know he were responsible somehow for the water mill down that way.

In Wooster, Dorothy Fangs – who could outwork a dozen menfolk to dying and bury them without mussing her apron.

The Ohio country had got spirits like the wood has panthers – more heard of than seen. But when you did see them, you recollected it all your life. I do not say these were all true spirits. But neither does that make them false. You never saw Boone or Crockett or Fink or Billy Earthquake Esquire either and they are in news papers and almanacs.

I have distracted myself. As I begun to tell, the promised tenderness cussedness and tragedy related to whether my brother were a merchant or merchandise or both. You will agree that a candy tastes sweeter when you steal it. There is a different taste for the storekeeper you stole from. Progress requires fetching more than you paid for a thing.

Now consider my brother as a trader. Recollect his first great offering of nine years before – his Sunday promise to clear ground for a city among the western trees. The flea-folks had only laughed at his offer to clear the woods in two days and a night. They went to bed still grinning at the jackassed idea. But they woke to see that Big had done it. Their mouths forgot how they had laughed and spoke poor of my brother, and went to licking their teeth over the good land. Thousands of acres to husband on – build on – live on – buy and sell on.

Big spread his hands out and said to them *Go ahead.* Not one soul thought about his open and empty palms as they ran to claim lots. Big did not think of his empty palms either. It were enough for him to be wondered at and adored.

In the Gospels you never hear of Christ doing carpenter work for wages. On the question of hard money, he only holds up a coin and says *This hasn't got my name on it any* and pitches it into the waters of Jordan. When Christ were borrowing Simon Peter's fishboat, I wonder if he were scooping up that same coin to do the trick on a fresh crowd of folks. I do not mean to call Christ a swindler. Only that making folks credence takes theatre grease, and it would have been costly to throw coins all day long.

It is pudding minded talking of my brother and Christ in the same breath. It is grabbing after the lowest branch. It is lazy work. I forgive myself. We have just got these ideas scratched into our brains.

You would not trust Christ to run a bank though. He would dump out all your money for the sick and weary-hearted.

At first Big did not mind his empty palms. Not when he whipped a lake. Nor when he lied to the devil – stalked the deepest woods – hogtied panthers – drained jugs – got stung by one thousand hornets and only smiled – cut roads – moved the mouth of the Cuyahoga – dug a canal – drained twenty swamps – rescued one hundred widows and several married men besides.

He has got more feats than you have got ears to hear, and he never asked a penny for them. Besides, what have you and your ears to pay for such a thing? What is the correct price of such merchandise?

So Big come to live on adoration – by slaps-on-his-back – by refreshment – by the flock of small fry that imitated him – by other folks' wonder. This arrangement were considered settled in ink by the citizens of Ohio city and Cleveland. The tenderness cussedness and tragedy come when Big decided it were not enough to be wondered at.

You know the advertisement by now. Big Son has rastled rivers and lakes and rescued women in woe. Met the devil twice and whipped him three times. Ate panther fricassee for breakfast and tiger steaks at supper. Taught wolves how to wail and put a face on the moon with a rusty musket. Big Son has done more feats than you have brains to hold et c.

For his next one he liked something else entirely. No

brawling or biting, and no empty palms after. For his next wonder Big wished to grab hold of the land as he had watched men do. To make a place of his own and populate it with shining-haired small fry. To quit being wondered at and start wondering on. To quit being loved up and start loving.

He wanted to be more flesh than spirit.

He wanted Miss Cloe.

You have not met many folks besides my brother and myself. I ought to start with Miss Cloe Inches. Recall that I said my brother never met any queens. Miss Cloe were not a queen. I do not consider *queen* is word enough.

Cloe Inches were an orphan raised in the house of Mr Job and Mrs Tab Stiles alongside my brother and myself – so she were our own somewhat-sister. I never known how Mr and Mrs Inches done apart from dying. She were between Big and myself in age, and sometimes mistaken for our blood kin. As pretty as Big were strong, and plenty strong herself. As tall as me, half a head shorter than Big. Hair of the darkest brown, just a breath short of black. Cheeks perpetually blushed, like the blood inside knew a private joke.

You would like such a creature to steal my brother's heart. But she were not agreeable to the role of bouncing bride. By her own nature and by the example of Mrs Tab Stiles, Cloe were not at all meek. Her birthday was in the month of June and summer thunderstorms stayed in her eyes all the year. She had manners mostly but she could out-rastle and outcuss most folks if you asked her to. She would outwork you without any asking at all.

My brother were a great hand for feats, but for steady habits there were no one better than Cloe Inches. She would keep after a task longer than Big or anyone you know, and no one ever stopped to pay her wonder. Cloe did not bother with prodigious *thwock*s – her work sounded more like *thk*, quiet and tidy. Big could juggle boulders all day, but Cloe would make candles – churn butter – stitch smocks – put dry clothes on the young Stileses – teach them school – butcher hogs and a hundred *thk*s more and then holler us in for supper. All while Big were only making a circus with rocks.

I do not say any lovers' secret when I tell that my brother meant to wed Cloe. He had said as much out loud and sober. He only wanted to convince her.

Big and Cloe and myself strolling in the lanes under a yolk-colored dusk. Children and dogs and day pigs running around and between us. Crickets sawing their fiddles. Past the gibbering of youth and insect you could hear how specially quiet Big gone.

Cloe   will you be married to me?

Big stopped still. Speaking such an idea and walking were too much at once.

Cloe walked on even as she answered. *Have you got a house for us to live in?*

Big made to catch up.   *I would build us one*

27

Would you build us money for a lot to raise it on?

My brother had a way of tilting his head when a truth bit him.

Big and Cloe and myself plucking deceased chickens in the cold January barn. With bits of feather dancing in the air, Big asked again.

Cloe   will you be married to me?

Cloe did not turn from her work. *What will you do to earn a keep?*

Big sat with his chicken and considered.

Big and Cloe and myself stringing popcorn for Washington's Birthday. His needle stopped ominously and it come out again.

Cloe   will you be married to me?

I do not consider you are marriageable, Big

Cloe   we will not want for a thing if only we make man and woman of each other

What have you got that will make me more of a woman?

He put his attention back to the popcorn.

Big and Cloe and myself whitewashing the backside of the house after the last of the snow were melted. The creatures in the barn watched curious from their stalls. Big drew a deep drink of air as he dunked his brush.

Cloe—

Big   I do not wish to be wed to anyone at all just now

Big come to be scorched severally – by his empty palms, and by Miss Cloe's considering that he were wanting in respects. In confidence I do not think my brother wore his best ears when making his proposals of marriage. He only heard the first bits of Cloe's spurning – that he were poor, that he were wanting prospects, et c. He did not hear the second bits of Cloe's being against marrying anyone at all just now. He took away from their lyceums the idea that he ought to secure an income, and that an income would secure Cloe, and so secure his happiness.

The only income Big had ever known was wonder won by feats. But by the coming of spring 1837, he had hunted out all Ohio city and Cleveland besides for feats wanting doing. There is only so much to do, even in a growing country. The yield of his work thinned out some too. There is only so much wonder in a place.

In the months of March and April Big turned sideways. He had shown before a tendency to create a mess in the making of a miracle. Now he went straight on to the mess without the miracle bit. Big Son who cut roads to nowhere. Who dug a well into dry rock. Who tried to rastle tame creatures. Who emptied jugs and went looking for brawls. Who tried to cure hog cholera.

My brother were not a doctor of swine or any creature. He somehow took sick with the hog cholera himself and puked enough to drown a horse. It were a feat but not the good sort.

There is a sickness worse than hog cholera, named despair. Big determined he would not succumb – that he would find remedy.

Spring.

Honest work is medicine. You cannot bottle or buy better remedy, whatever your ailment. On the first day of spring 1837, Mr Big Son determined to physic himself.

Our days proceeded somewhat like birds. You cannot rely on birds for any exact behavior, but you seen patterns in their doing. Sniff the wind some – fly around – make hidys at your cousins – swoop down and poke at corncobs. It is fool behavior, but regular. Do anything regular enough, and it becomes sacrament.

You cannot rely on a day entirely but you know the sun will come up.

On the first day of spring, that sun found us in our attic apartments above the Stiles barn. With the sun came the birds for a sing at our hayloft door. Those little birds peeked in at a long low room. Two straw beds and plenty of blankets. Two chairs. A few souvenirs of Big's rambunctions. His red neckerchief hung on a nail.

A dozen birds come out for that day's choir. Some of the singers come right into the attic to consider the crumbs and other savories that resided in Big's bedclothes. My brother ate prodigiously, at all hours. You could practically hear hunger grumbling inside his snores, just before a grand brass yawn of *snnnnChhtFppth* announced that Big had joined the day. He shook his limbs out of his blankets and shooed off the scavenging birds, although one brave sparrow lingered to tug at a bone.

Another eyeful of my brother – let us see him close. At four and twenty years he had the bones of a man but the demeanor of a boy still. He were strong all over, such that even his shining brown hair and his ivory teeth seemed to have muscles. His eyes was somewhat small and close, and they tinied up to nothing when he laughed – a cannon sound that could rout any misery.

A roaring yawn and a thumping of the chest. *Today is the day, little brother*, he pronounced. *I will make an honest man of myself*

First, he would make his toilet. He picked up his sliver of looking glass and fussed some with his hair. Tied on his red neckerchief – sleep were the only place you could find him without it. Once the kerchief were on, he were open to custom. Without another blink, he dove down into the yard of the Stiles homeplace.

* * *

There was a ladder down from the attic, but most days Big preferred to leap into the barnyard. On this day he landed in a mudhole occupied by the sow Arabella, who thrown one eye open to hidy Big and gone back to sleep. Next to greet him were the chickens, who clucked their hidys as they fled from his stomping across the yard.

From the kitchen came the next hulloa of

MIND YOUR FOOTING, BIG

Mrs Tabitha Stiles known from experience that Big were already dripping mud and soon to kick something over. Even as Big hidyed back, he tumbled over a pail. Mrs Tab's head shot out from the half door of the kitchen and eyed my brother like he were a mess to clean – like her stare were soap.

Despite the hard looks, Mrs Tabitha had an abundance of love for us. Only that she gone about loving like wringing the head off a chicken – best do it fast and hard. Her mothering were almost ferocious. Food were an example. She would get a corncake in your mouth as soon as you come within her reach. Often you did not even mark her approach with the corncake – she struck like a panther.

As Big drew up a bucket of water from the well Mrs Tab come after him with the first cake of the day. Even as Big chewed his breakfast, he spoke, scattering crumbs to the chickens.

Today is the day, Mrs Tab
I expect it is, Big
Today is the day I find honest work

She gone after him with another cake. I believe there were times when she fed a person only to keep them from talking.

I will never be useless anymore, Mrs Tab   A shower of crumbs and another *Today is the day* like he were convincing himself.

Judging from her aspect – if I imagine her mind – Mrs Tab were not sure God had made Big to be useful – not sure anyone in history had ever been useful enough.

But all she said to Big were *While you are making yourself useful   take that busted harness to Mr Philo*

Big climbed on the tall bay Agnes and went toward usefulness at a walk – just as I come down the ladder looking for my own day's work. I waved at Big's back and greeted the other creatures – a hulloa to the pigs and chickens, a scratch between the ears for Asa the ox – and submitted to my corncakes from Mrs Tab. I did not find Mr Job in the yard or barn, so I went into the homeplace.

Can you see the Stiles homeplace?

Two rooms, one sat on top of the other – the upper for sleeping, the lower for every other chore. A front door faced the lane but were never used – everyone known to call at the kitchen door in the back, which looked out on our barn. In our younger years Big and Cloe and I had slept in the homeplace with Mr Job and Mrs Tab. But as their natural children multiplied and Big took to the occasional night-fry, we migrated to our attic for propriety and comfort. Cloe

34

slept in the homeplace still, as the governess of the seven little Stileses.

Job Jr age fourteen – John twelve – Jonah ten – Joseph called Joe eight – Josiah six – Jomes called Jom four – and little Joy two.

I found the entire regiment gathered in the downstairs for morning lessons. As I come into the kitchen door I saw Cloe's back, and before her the seven little ones sat on three coffins laid out as pews.

We favored coffins for sitting on account of Mr Job's work.

You will say it is morbid to have coffins for furniture.

It is only good sense.

The first hour of the day was set aside for a shouting-school. Their little hands would be set to chores but not before moral and mental improvement. Cloe were leading the seven through their alphabets by a memory game – they were to remember a Bible person for every letter.

J? said Cloe.

Six *Jesus*es and a babble from little Joy.

And what did Jesus do?

He made miracles, said Joe on behalf of the assembly.

K?

Seven silences.

Never mind K   L?

La-za-russ, said the older young ones. *Lab-ar-aaa,* said the younger young ones, and a breath later Joy added *zarss*

And how did Lazarus do?

The sound of small brains churning. *He died but Jesus woke up him* said Job Jr. *He got doctored* added Josiah, thoughtful.

Good   Now the letter M?

Meed! I yelled from the behind them.

You are not a Bible mister shrieked Jom.

Don't stand there and watch Meed   it makes me itch

Itch or no, Cloe went along with my fooling. *And how does Mr Meed do?*

Myself I mostly helped Mr Job with the coffins. You can live without a coffin but you cannot die without one – make it a coffin from Stiles and go in style.

I apologize for the Yankee peddler talk – it is a habit of enterprise.

Coffins is what kept the family fed and watered. In a shop at the back corner of the barn, Mr Job and I knocked together burying boxes and other small furnitures. You might startle to hear of a coffin called furniture but give it thought. A good coffin will do as a bench – a chest of linens – a sideboard if you stack two – a wardrobe if you turn it on end – it has even got rope handles for easy transport. The idea is keen thrift – you are expecting to be buried by 1850, or 1860 if you are careful of your health. Consider what a good coffin will cost in twenty years' time. You can cinch yours at the 1837 price or swap us a shoat. You get a chiffoneer into the bargain. I never like to see a neighbor buried but better for them to ride in Stiles. We bring the box to you – fill it however you like.

As the school lesson moved from Meed to Nebuchadnezzar, Mr Job stuck his long goose's neck into the kitchen door.

Hitch up Asa   We have got deliveries

You ought to meet the monarchs of the manger.

Big loved Cloe most but he loved Agnes first. She were a tall bay mare, good hearted and headstrong. She were also a fiend for grooming. You never saw such vanity in a creature. Agnes would grab a brush in her nimble teeth and drop it at your feet. If you did not take the suggestion, she might bite after your ears until you heard her. Once, I swear, Agnes brought me silk ribbons in her teeth – she meant for me to tie them into her mane.

Another vanity – Agnes would not work beside another horse or mule. She did not care for the company of other creatures at all, apart from Asa.

Agnes were hardly the only one partial to Asa the ox. He were the most congenial citizen of Ohio, known and loved by folks in every corner of the city. I do not think it strange to say that Asa were my good friend. He had the heart of a four-legged dog, would follow you on chores and supply good company. Even the swing of his hindquarters had cheer in it.

Those hindquarters was particularly galvanized that morning, and we near to flew along even with a dozen coffins

piled on the wagon. The bustle of Ohio city at day's beginning. Hammers and hoes falling like birdsong – progress
gnawing the very air. We swapped hulloas with neighbors
as we gone, and a few loose dogs and day pigs chased along
to greet Asa. We rolled past churches and jail and the
steam-powered chair factory, which Mr Job held in disdain –
coffins were good enough for sitting, and hands enough for
working. Past the office block and the *ARGUS* news paper
and rope walk and a dozen stores spilling their wares out
onto the street like cracked eggs.

There is no quiet season for coffin work. Folks generally
die when it suits them. You could make a burying box with
confidence that it would find filling before long, and merchants on both sides of the river had standing orders for
Stiles readymades on account of the fever season coming.
With a Stiles readymade, all you want is nails mallet and
shovel. I suppose you also want a deceased person and a
preacher as well.

The latter items you have to find yourself. But you could
fetch up the *nails mallet and shovel* and a thousand notions
more from Handerson and Panderson, foremost merchants
and our first delivery of the day. Asa hardly needed steering
to take us to H and P – he knew from habit that a candy
awaited him there. Asa were incorrigible on the question of
sugar. There had been instances of his looking into private
windows and doors if he sniffed sweets. Even as I hitched
him up outside the merchants', I saw a madman look in his
great brown eyes.

As Mr Job untied the ropes around the boxes, I ducked into the cool darkness of the emporium – a man-made wilderness of merchandise. Barrels stuffed with tools and garlands strung with bedpans. Dressmakings and hats and cheeses hanging overhead between shelves groaning with bottles of I do not know what. You felt lost in all the possibility. From somewhere inside the thicket, I heard either Handerson or Panderson greet me.

Hulloa, sir

It were a trick to tell their voices apart.

We have got a mile of new calicoes bug bane congress water milk of roses a score of Newyork shirts a gross of good clay pipes

Telling Handerson from Panderson did not matter to anyone but their wives. They were two fleshes with a single mind.

Broadcloth Linen and worsted drillings Worked collars and capes A carefully selected assortment of family groceries The very best of teas and old java coffee Raisins

You can see their single mind had a single idea.

Sheeting and shirting Very choice carpets and rugs Tobacc—

This would go on if you did not bust in.

Coffins are here

Before my lips were still, a long thin arm – Handerson's – shot out from a heap of bonnets, clutching a peppermint stick for Asa.

*

A memory told to me by Mr Job. As a boy Mr Philo Fish were a maniac for speed. He run through meals and run through chores and even run the words out of his mouth in a startled chirrup. Philo were at perpetual rebellion against standing still. He were not running away, but only preferred as much dispatch as he could get – in line with the national attitude. Why walk when you might run?

He raced that way through fifteen years until a horse dropped dead on top of him. The weight of the deceased broke Philo's right leg up and down. No more running for a time. Bed rest did not suit Philo and he did not give his leg time to heal proper. It proved that the leg were weary of Philo's *huphup*, and took gangrene rather than go back to running everywhere. It were deemed best that the boy and his leg part ways. At their farewell, the surgeon poured some whiskey over his implement and handed the jug to the boy for courage.

Philo drank down half of the jug and has been racing through them since.

He never much mourned the leg, which Pa Fish wanted to bury with Christian manners. Philo only said to *give it to the night pigs* and took up learning leatherwork. Ever since he has made a calling from rigging harnesses and saddles and every other notion that kept a horse or other creature in place. Folks knew better than to pity Philo for his lameness. He would spit on that.

* * *

Big and Agnes made a straight line to Mr Philo's shop with the busted harness. Today were the day for rigging the whole world.

Hidy Phi

Mr Philo hidyed back by a froggy belch. Partly from whiskey and partly from nature, Philo lacked for parlor manners.

Mrs Tabitha would have this harness fixed up   Big held the harness up like it were meat for the pot.

Philo were getting around on his one natural leg and a cane. He liked to save his false leg for formal occasions. By a tilt of his head he instructed Big to add the harness to a pile in the corner. Big done as he were told and turned back – meaning to ask Mr Philo to take him as an apprentice.

Instead he were struck in the chest with a pair of shoes.

Take those to the Dog and fetch me back the jugs he swapped me
I surely will, Phi

As Big slung the shoes over his neck, he engined his courage up some.

And I might   say   another word to you   Phi

Big never wore hats on account of vanity of his hair, but he still reached up like he were removing an imaginary one out of respect. Agnes looked in from the open window as if to encourage Big's asking.

Mr Fish

Philo had not been paying him any mind since throwing the shoes. He were taking a loud p___ into one of his empty jugs. After an awful long time Mr Philo finished with a cere-monial *braraapgh* and clomped back to his workbench.

What is it Big? Philo were still holding the jug of his own water.

Now my brother came unstuck— *Mr Philo I have gotto-havemoneytowedCloe   I will work for it   Have you gotwork-forme?   Teach me leatherwork Mr Philo   You have known me since I were a tadpole   Have you work for me?*

Mr Philo set down the jug of p___ slow and scratched behind his ear.

I was wondering if you ever meant to hitch Cloe up

I mean to Phi I do   To make a wife of her and a honest man of myself

Mind your wishes

Big twisted his lips around to grab the next words. Before he found any, Philo answered.

I haven't got s___ for you to do

Big shrunk down some.

And if I did have s___, I would not give it   You have got a higher purpose than to sit and fart all day, Big

It were no puzzle to tell Handerson from Panderson with your eyes. Handerson were as skinny as a foal's legs and Pan-derson were just the opposite. It were round Panderson that came charging out of the emporium to direct Mr Job and me as we unloaded the order of coffins.

*SET THEM ON END THERE   LIKE THEY ARE STANDING UP
TO GREET FOLKS   IF YOU WOULD*

As soon as we had one stood up, it were Handerson writing on it with a chalk – Panderson had vanished back into the thicket in pursuit of a customer. As Handerson bent from the waist to scrawl the price of FOUR DOLLARS on the coffin, he looked like a vast grasshopper – even his green suitclothes encouraged the likeness.

Mr Job looked troubled by thoughts as we stood up the next coffin.

Handerson—

It were round Panderson back again somehow, puffing at a cigar.

—Panderson   you have got your numbers wrong   You are selling these for less than you paid for them

From inside a round cloud come THE READYMADE COFFINS IS ONLY TO LOOSEN UP POCKETBOOKS ONCE A MAN THINKS HE HAS A BARGAIN, HE LOSES HIS DISCERNMENT

Mr Job had a particular silence he took when he thought a person foolish. I could see him buttoning that silence on, plain as Panderson's smoke. As we tied up the remaining load, Mr Job forgot his silence to hidy Miss Sarahjoseph gliding past, her feet hidden in skirts. She were the maid of Mr Clark, the richest man in Ohio.

Mr Job   Mr Meed   Mr Panderson— Each name came with a violent curtsy of the neck.

Back came Handerson, bowing in his grasshopper way,

nearly putting his nose to the front of Sarahjoseph's bonnet.

MA'AM ATYOURSERVICE MA'AM   WE HAVE GOT MILES OF CALI—

Oh it is alright Mr Handerson   I do not need the whole show   I am only come for more brandied fruits   Mr Clark is gustatory today

Big tied Mr Dog Dogstadter's shoes together by the laces and hung them over his neck. Asking Philo was only practice. Only a puddingbrain would give up hunting after one poor miss. His next shot were ready at hand – Philo's closest neighbor, Mr Ozias Basket the teamster. Big walked Agnes across the lane and hitched her at the rail, where she sniffed mule scent with disdain.

Inside the Basket barn, the mules added their jabbering to the stink. They was domiciled in long rows on each side, and as Big gone down the wide center, the creatures made loud hulloas. He found Mr Ozias in the very last stall.

Oze Basket were uncommonly tidy for a man of his trade, put that same maniac tidiness on his mules. So it were not unusual that Big found the proprietor brushing the teeth of the mule Absalom – all the mules had respectable Bible names painted in white on their stall, although they was largely heathens.

Hidy Mr Oze   Big went after his invisible hat again.

Hidy Big   Oze had a voice like rust.

44

A long moment passed with Mr Ozias holding the brush to Absalom's denture.

What luck of mine brings you here?

A hesitation. *Oze   I   am   consideringmystationinlife   and I havedecideditistime   that I come honest   done regular work for regular profit*

Oze let another moment limp past.   *Glad to know it Big*

The conversation perished entirely – even the mules quieted. Eventually Big scratched thoughtfully behind an ear and took his leave.

Mean Mr Ozias could not discourage Big. Besides, Oze were well-known for stinting with money. Mr Ozias were only neighbors to Mr Philo and Big had only stopped for practicality. That were all.

Next door to the Basket barn was the offices of Dr Strickland, the cherrycheeked dentist – from mule's teeth to folks'. Big found Dr S in the midst of fitting YL Honey with a new and incorruptible denture. Big sheeped some on account of he had been the one who wrecked YL's previous denture in a rastle. But he managed a respectful hidy and YL hidyed back the best he could with Dr S's hand in his trap. No resentments was noted. The rastle had been a fair fight and not the first set of teeth YL had busted besides. YL were the unluckiest man in Ohio, suffering past his portion from misadventure, and learned to meet poor fortune with grace.

Big were improving at asking after work. *Dr S, I am here to—*

Beg patience, Big   Mr Honey and I have reached the decisive moment   The kreosote will sanitize the necrosis and provide purchase for the apparatus   The dentist pulled a brush from his smock and dipped it in a pot of stinking liquid.

This will bite some, friend

He daubed at YL's gums and stood back. The kreosote went to work and YL kicked his legs madly. Big and the dentist watched burly YL writhe in agony for a minute or more, before Dr S passed him a jug to rinse.

Now Mr Honey   it is imperative that you do not smoke any cigars or pipes the rest of the morning   The treatment is liable to ignite

As Dr S scrubbed up he listened to Big's proposition with a kindness. *Big if I had a spare dollar I would surely cut you a bite from it but—*

Big opened up his mouth some like he were expecting that bite of dollar. Dog's shoes hung around his neck like he had grown donkey's ears.

—I haven't got any spare dollar Big   You are better suited to busting teeth than carpentering them   I do appreciate how you bring me custom   You have a higher purpose besides   Take heart at that!

YL gave a *hrrmmh* of agreement without parting his new teeth, and slapped Big on the back.

Big left Dr S and swore he would not lose heart.

He called at Mr Dennes's.

He called at Handerson and Panderson.

He called at folks with no prospects at all.

The chair factory. The docks. The rope walk. The pottery. The ash pits. He even asked preachers if they needed deputies.

You can imagine how every such interview gone.

I haven't got enough dollars lying around for my own self
 Gold is powerful scarce this season Rascal Vanburen
  If anything shakes out you are the first I will think of
   You ought to take to farming
    You might speculate in land
     I would help you but I am awful skinned
     You are meant for spirit's work

With every turning away Big's pride shrunk some like old garments. By the end of the morning his self-regard were pinching some at his underarms and betweenlegs.

He had not wanted to

He did not want to

He preferred not to

He would call on rich Mr Clark at the site of his great bridge-to-be.

PROCEEDINGS CONCERNING THE CONSTRUCTION OF A BRIDGE OVER THE CUYAHOGA RIVER JANUARY 1837

ASKED what a bridge would cost.

COMMITTEE thinks *not more than twenty thousand dollars.*

ASKED who could pay so much.

GENERAL SILENCE.

MR CLARK: *Out of an abiding interest in the future of our two cities I will build the bridge and keep it in perpetuity free without toll.*

CONSIDERABLE APPLAUSE.

ASKED where the bridge ought to go.

MR CLARK: *At the Columbus road in the river flats.*

CONSIDERABLE CUSSING from Ohio city deputation.

OBSERVED that there is no good road up the hill there.

MR CLARK: *I will cut a road at my expense for the public good.*

CUSSING continued.

COMMENTED that *Cleveland will hog up all the wagons from the farm roads.*

COMMENTED that *Ohio city will have no cash or commerce.*

COMMENTED that *this bridge is wicked.*

MR CLARK ACCUSED of having interest in lots at the river bottom across from cussed bridge.

MR CLARK ACCUSED of vilest speculation.

MR CLARK *will not listen to such rubbish talk.*

SUGGESTED by Cleveland factions that Ohio city can build a second bridge if they spit on the first one.

SUGGESTED that second bridge be built at the site of the old floating bridge near Division- and Centre-streets.

SOME APPLAUSE.

ASSERTED by property owners from near Division- and Centre-streets that they will not have a bridge there on account of it being a nuisance to river traffic and the greater good.

RENEWED CUSSING.

MOVED TO ADJOURN if folks do not have more questions.

ASKED *what else would you hog after the farm wagons.*

ASKED *why do you wish to sin against us.*

ASKED *why ought we tolerate such abuse.*

ASKED *how would it be if we tore up your bridge.*

ASKED *may we borrow a bucket of your blood.*

OHIO CITY DEPUTATION HEARD TO CHANT *Two bridges or none* for a time.

COMMITTEE thinks this conduct is not respectable.

COMMITTEE asks that we have order.

CHANTING OF *Two bridges or none* continued.

You have marked these *bridge questions* and are curious—

This bridge of Mr Clark's – is it a special bridge?

No, a regular bridge, wood and stone, with two covered stretches and a draw in between.

So how did there come to be so many questions about a simple bridge?

Even after forty years of settlement at Cleveland and ten years at Ohio city, there were no bridge across the river. Because there were no obvious place for a crossing, and no wish to stand the cost. I consider the questions was less about the bridge than the river itself.

What is the nature of the river?

The river is mostly water with some dirt and fishes mixed in. The questions is more about its restless shape. Let me show you a picture-drawing.

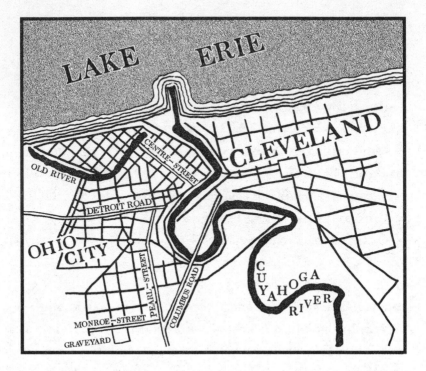

The head of the river is to our east, and the water runs
south, but somehow ends up northwest. At the last bit the
river goes rambunctious, and staggers all over the bottom
land between the bluffs of Cleveland and Ohio city. As a
consequence the two places are not neatly parted. There
are places in the river flats where you would go west from
Ohio city to reach Cleveland in the east – or nearly any
other direction.

At the Ohio city iron foundry at Centre-street, east were
straight south.

At Scranton's peninsula, east were north-northwest.

At the Columbus road, east were north.

The Columbus road is where rich Mr Clark put his bridge.

The *where* brung considerable heartache.

The river flats was the shared boiling heart of the two cities. Where road river canal and lake met and mixed all their blood. I read in the news paper that just one month brought *108 059 bushels wheat 988 555 pounds bacon 317 081 pounds lard* through the warehouses along the last mile of the Cuyahoga.

From boats come iron tools, oils and medicines, gunmeal, kegs of nails, linens and calicoes, lyes, salt, pots of grease, crockery, brandied fruits, news papers and notions. From wagons come goose feathers, oats, peas, beans, barley, pigs, beeswax and corn. From everywhere come people – emigrants, farmers and merchants. Full of doubt and debt and expectations. And purses for us to feed from.

The Columbus road came out of the fat farm country and ran along the western bluff into Ohio city, looking down over the flats. Mr Clark had not waited for any vote of approval or assent after making his pledge, but had set workmen to rip open the bluff right at the Columbus road. Through the first months of 1837, Clark's gangs cut a wide and easy road down the hill, and then set to work on a bridge. When it were done, all the plump wagons from the farm country would roll down the hill straight into Cleveland, and never into Ohio city at all – starving the little sister of commerce and custom.

*

As Big rode down to see Mr Clark, he chewed over what he would say. He were so lost in thinking that Agnes had to steer herself around the mudholes. At the crook of the hill, Mr Clark's bridge come into view below. Even half built you could not call it ugly. Two hundred feet long and wide enough for three wagons abreast. Two covered stretches and in between a draw for letting through masted boats. From afar it resembled two houses, end to end, set atop the water. The bald wood of the bridge had the look of cake, dotted with raisins, or flies – workmen crawling the top and sides, swinging hammers and saws.

Big swung off Agnes and gone to the closest of the workmen.

Now, you have not met any citizens of Cleveland yet. Here is your first. It is a trick to tell apart a Cleveland man from an Ohio city man. They look the same and generally act the same. The only difference is that Clevelanders are wrong all over. Too much Connecticut in them. Big were more genial toward Clevelanders than most Ohioans. But the workers he approached did not return the curtsy.

Hulloa there
A grunt.
Do you know where I could find Mr Clark to speak with him?
No
Thank you kindly

* * *

Hidy

A narrowing of eyes.

Where might I find Mr Clark?

A cautious consideration of this visitor with shoes hung around his neck. *Ask the foreman*

Mister   yes   hidy

The smallest hitch in the swing of a hammer.

Are you the foreman?   I wish to see the foreman

What do you want?

I want a position

Haven't got any of those

Is Mr Clark about?

A hammer pointed to the Cleveland side of the river.

Under the noon-fat sun, Big led Agnes across the half-made bridge, their six feet and eight shoes mindful of the unfinished bits where the river showed through. The bridge had a gentle slope down from west to east, and the flats spread out like a table before my brother. A short ways off from the bridge were a pompous elm and underneath were Mr Clark, clad in a suit of barking white linen. His considerable self rested on a folding stool, with one hand on a knee and the other holding a long fork. Attending him were Miss Sarahjoseph, back from Handerson and Panderson with her basket full of brandied fruits.

Big! Mr Clark bellowed. *Big Son!   A welcome surprise   Most welcome*

Hidy Mr Clark   Miss Sarahjoe

A sharp, short curtsy.

Come in comeincomein, Mr Clark said in a food-clotted voice.

Big were not sure how to come in considering they were out of doors.

Sit sit sitsitsit said Mr Clark as he went into a fresh jar of peaches with his fork.

Mr Clark had the way of some rich folks of acting as if they are the same as you. He seemed tickled to audience with Big. He wiped up his chops with a kerchief even whiter than his suit, and pushed the jar of peaches at his caller. Big fished a slice out with his fingers, to be courteous.

Their interview commenced.

Mr Clark I want to   make a honest life for myself—

Commendable   most commendable Another stab at the jar.

—but I want for means—

Gustation.

—and I wonder if you would take me on a worker at your bridge   It is mostly done   but you know my appetite   I could build a dozen bridges for you   do anything for you   rastle alligators for you   if you have any alligators

Big I am proud to hear of your turning honest   I am boiled pink—

Big were unsure how it signified to be boiled pink.

—but I cannot give you work

My brother's face fell off.

54

—on account of Progress   We are Progressing as a People and a Place   With each "P," Mr Clark sent molecules of fruit flying.   *Your feats brung us a long ways toward Progress   You have already done so much for us   We cannot have you do more   We must stand on our own*

Big worked to pull his face back on, but it did not fit right.

Mr Clark paused with a gob of peach on the end of his fork. He considered some. There was a genuine boiled-pinkness to him. You could not say if it were from the liquor in the fruit or from tenderness at the hero's predicament.

Big   my word to you   once the bridge is done   once my money is unhitched from it   I will fix you in paying work   I will see it done

On Pearl-street, Asa snorted to a stop in front of DOGSTAD-TER GROCER. Folks mostly just called this place Dog's. The oldest and most ragged public place on the west side of the Cuyahoga, run by an old and ragged person. The sign promised a grocery but the only good for sale was whiskey. Dog did not come out to greet us, but several of the cats what roosted in his establishment stepped outside to hulloa Asa. As the cats rubbed their brains on his ankles, Asa shook flies out of his ears. Mr Job and I went to unloading the last of the day's load.

COFFINS   I hollered.

Bring the f____s in   Dog hollered back.

* * *

The inside of the grocery was always dusk, no matter the hour. A long slender room with little pig-eye windows at the entrance. The air sogged with smoke and drink-breath and cat-fur and the heat of a half dozen stoves. Along the walls between stoves were a chaos – whiskey makings – busted pieces of barrel – animal hides and broken coffin-bits and news papers and soiled books.

Long galley tables filled the room, dotted with idlers and loafers – some asleep – some at checkers – some simply talking without any listener. They all sat on good Stiles coffin-benches. Between the seething stoves and mumbling drunks and mayowing cats there were a wormy music to the place.

The decorations helped along the wormy feeling. Above the heaps of junk, the walls bristled with violence. Hoes, plows, rakes, scythes. Mattocks and sledges. Pokers and tongs. Mammoth laundry spoons and rusted cleavers. Implements for encouraging people. Pikes, clubs, a spear, war hatchets, aged muskets. At the center of the back wall were the prize, a rheumy sword. Its liverspotted blade would not pierce boiled beef, but it did cut a style.

Under the sword were ancient August Dogstadter, barely two feet from the largest of the stoves, perched on a stick stool. His bare feet kicked before him – Dog often kicked in the middle of talking, like it helped along his point.

—*and he busted the gallows*   *They had fed him so much whis-*

key before hanging   at his request   that no one known if he were
dead or only pissbrained   They did not wish to bury him living so
they only left him tucked under the broken gallows for a few hours to see

Dog were a considerable success as a whiskey grocer, but his true gift lie in spinning wild stories from between his frightful teeth – jagged and green.

—and then that night, the sheriff said to the doctors   <u>Do to</u>
<u>his carcass as you like</u>   <u>only do not make much noise</u>—

Some was lies on history.

—and John Omic were awfully fat   too fat for one man to
carry   but a drunk Dr Allen took it as a challenge and hoisted
him on his back   And made way only to trip over a stump—

Some was lies on his own prowess.

—In my summer I were strong enough to hoist fat old Omic and
dance a jig under him—

Some was lies for amusement.

—but down gone burly Dr Allen with the fat f_____g dead man
on top of him like blankets and the other doctors could not laugh
aloud on account of being graverobbers—

Some was lies so strange and dark I could not say what they were for.

—but it turned out Omic weren't at all dead   he coughed and
puked and pleaded   Dr Allen pissed himself in fright—

I had heard the story of John Omic, the first man hung in Cleveland, many times before.

—and then the doctors had to stab Omic in the heart to keep
their graverobbing a secret even if their carcass   weren't even a

carcass and Dr Allen stood up covered in piss and puke and Indian blood

Dog's stories never ended but with him laughing – a sound like beating dust from a rug.

Job Stiles   do you mark how they are f____g us?

There were no confusing who *they* was and how they effed Dog. The question of the bridge had termited Dog's brains since January, when rich Mr Clark had declared his plan to build a crossing at the Columbus road.

I do not consider Clark's bridge wrongs me any   said Mr Job.

That is because you are a sow's marital parts *Job Stiles   You was born that way*

Dog did not say *marital parts*. He said a different word that I will not put down. From any but Dog, such talk would have chased Mr Job away. But Dog's manners was like the smallpox – if you survived, you were cured for life.

I would wager you, Dog   a whole penny   that Cleveland and Ohio are destined to wed into a single city one day   and when it happens, you will wonder why you minded   Mr Job said.

I will be ruined long before then   with no farmers to pour whiskey into   Ruined if I am not already riding in one of your boxes   I have set your swap barrel at the door   Have a drink to grease your wagon wheels

The hour were just noon but hauling coffins were drying work. Over a sip, Dog and Mr Job lyceumed about Mr Clark's bridge and just how it were sinning on us, and I read through a news paper.

In this number of the *ARGUS* there were an account of a sea serpent seen at the coast of Maine. I wished there were a drawing of the serpent. You cannot trust a news paper every time. If that serpent were real and cared to visit Ohio I would pay to see it. I knowed Big would relish a chance to rastle such a monster.

Just as soon as I thunk of Big, my brother thunk himself through the door, bearing Dog's shoes and a smile like his teeth wanted to bust out and dance.

From Phi He held up the shoes like he had hunted them. *Refresh me before you finally drop dead* The shoes flown across the grocery and scattered several cats.

Drink up you piece of night soil Dog eagerly tugged on a repaired shoe. *I will lose one of these in your ass one sunny day*

Dog and Big relished jawing. Big and everyone else used Dog and Dog's grocery as a sanitary device – letting out words we could never spill elsewhere.

Mr Job *Little brother* A jug pull – a glance at my news paper – Big were not much for literature. *I have brung my own news*

A few seconds trickled past before Mr Job obliged him with *What news have you got Big?*

Mr Clark has promised me work

    God's grand design revealed said Mr Job.

      What happiness said I.

        Lardhearted f_____ said Dog.

He has promised me a position and I will have a wage and a prospect and a Cloe

* * *

A general congratulations was made and toast raised all around the room. But even as I clapped Big on the back, his mention of Cloe bit me some. We all belonged to each other as brothers and sister. I did not like to imagine Cloe belonging to him alone. He had enough already. I were happy to notice Mr Job's shroud of silence – of judgment not spoken – was back on him.

Dog did not wear any shroud. He merrily hissed that – wage and prospect and Cloe aside – Big *will never come to* night soil *You are no man only a spirit A chickenpuke fancy* This were a kick aimed right for a bruise.

But Big only struck up the churchorgan laugh. *They will bury you soon enough, but your charms will live forever A drink to the Dog*

The celebratory loafing did not last long before Mr Job announced *we had better get home dry or risk a hiding by mother Tab*

The return to day's light stung our eyes. Cleaner air was welcome though. A hulloa to patient Asa and Agnes, hitched together. A pile of crap behind them told how long we had been at idling. On the ride home the empty wagon clattered merrily.

At the homeplace Mrs Tab come after us again with the corncakes. She must have found our smell suspicious, but she did not withhold our cakes. As we chewed she shared the town talk.

60

You just missed Sarahjoe just gone   She has want of a bury-ing box

I seen her at Handerson and Panderson's this very morn-ing   She might have had one there

She wants a large one on account of Mr Clark's stoutness

I am not a doctor but I am generally expert with noticing. So I will wager an explanation for Mr Clark's fatal rupture – the brandied fruits done for my brother. Many folks so stricken was known to eat brandied fruits soon before. You will not catch me eating any.

At hearing the news, I hoped that Mr Clark were far-ing better than Dives from the Bible. Too much richness takes a body past mending. We said some Christian words for Mr Clark's soul, and somewhere in the sorrow Big van-ished without a word.

After dinner, a peaceful hour around the fire – seven Stiles children studying their marbles – Mrs Tab and Cloe sewing intently – Mr Job reading from the Psalms *All they that go down to dust shall bow before Him and none can keep alive his own soul –* for me a chew and whittling – Big remained absent.

Just before I bedded down, Big finally come to the roost. His light were dimmed some with drink, though his mouth were burning bright. He were mourning the deceased, except the mourning seemed more to do with his own expectations than Mr Clark's.

He unburdened himself of the entire saga of his day. At Dog's, he had only told the happy part. But now he unfurled his entire beggar's tour of Ohio city – his humbling – his hearing over and over that he were *meant for better work* – his brief triumph and sudden fall.

I allowed he had a worse day than all but Mr Clark.

I could not even ask Cloe to marry me during the hour I were marriageable

I did not speak my judgment that Cloe would not have found him any more marriageable. I only put the candle to sleep.

Straw rustling and the snoring of Asa and Agnes and other creatures below, and great fitful sighs from across the attic.

Little brother

It were no use to pretend sleep. Big would talk at a tree stump when the mood come on.

Big

Little brother   did you hear what the Dog said today?

About putting a shoe in your ass

About I were only a spirit and not a man

He were just cussing you

What if he were sneaking truth in cusses?   What if I am only a spirit?   What if I am another Chapman?

We are not too starchy here. It takes a great deal to offend a westerner. But John Appleseed Chapman were past pardoning. He dressed in such rags that you could see through to his privates. His beard were matted up into felt. Even his gifts of apple seed seemed untoward. He wore a chamber-pot on his head and I doubt he remembered the last time he went to bed sober.

Chapman visited us long ago, before any of Big's feats, before the incident that put the spirit on him, before the west side had more than a few folks. Big and I were small. On account of Chapman's reputation as the patron of orchards, the settlement of Cleveland put on a celebra-tory feed. Chapman did not eat a bite – only drank awful amounts. His very presence put an itch on you, like you were dressed in winter clothes at summer. The more we seen of Chapman the more we wanted shut of him. After he got too hospitable toward a young maid, some of the men encouraged him to move along. His scent stayed on for some days.

Chapman showed that a spirit of the times is not an incor-ruptible thing. Not hooped with iron. Not immune from rust or rodents. There were others like him. In Lorain, their Large Dutch had turned wild like a night pig – hollering in German about no one known what – robbing farmers. Near Hinckley folks feared to meet Feathers, in his gown made of buzzards – he stole children. Dick of Norwalk lived under-water and ate sailors. Stinking Squirrelcoat of the woods, et c.

Chapman and all those proved that spirits did have a ten-dency to go sideways – though Big were surely not as sideways as Chapman. The man had had a democratic use in his prime – spreading the hygienic drink of cider – but by the time of my encounter, he were all chewed up.

I had thought on Big's question before he asked it that night. What kind of spirit were Big? When is a spirit's work finished? What comes after?

It were only the third day of spring but the stoves at Dog's grocery made an indoors summer. I were already dabbing at my brow before the preacher said a word. But fat Mr Clark did not mind the close air any on account of being dead. The undertaker had gone after him with powders and paint such that he looked like a Philadelphia actor.

I do not speak ill of the departed when I say Mr Clark had a vanity. He cared for clothes and niceties – even now he rode on a masterpiece of a coffin by Mr Job, oak polished to pearl. It were a shame to give it to the worms beneath the Monroe-street burying ground. The rich man were vain of attention too, and it carried on past dying. His will said to spread him out in a public place, but not a church, so folks could have refreshment, and better to keep women home. The will went on to say you ought to read the rest of me aloud for any that cared to hear in that same public place, before you even bury him.

You might recollect certain intemperances from Dog regarding Mr Clark – regarding the deceased having lard for a heart et c. They never was friends or on visiting terms, but Dog never missed a chance to draw custom. So he had offered up his grocery as the public place, and loyal Sarahjoe had draped the room with crepe beforehand, out of Mr Clark's love of upholstery. It were a sight to see the grocery done up. Sarahjoe had even gone after the cats and tied mourning ribbons around their necks.

A burial wanted manners – wanted passing by the coffin under Dog's wall of weapons with your head bare. Substantial folks from both sides of the river was in attendance – mayors Frawley of Ohio and Willey of Cleveland. Factory owners and landlords and merchants and every other man of means. They puffed at pipes and spat tobacco politely, while Dog spidered around pouring whiskey and cussing less than usual.

The reverence were not all on account of manners. Mr Clark's will would include his bridge. It was expected that the bridge would become property of the public interest – though which public and which interest remained to be told.

Before the manners wore out, stout short Mayor Frawley stood up at the front of the grocery to read out the will. He had tobacco crusted at the corners of his mouth and looked already worse off for drink, but he and everyone else were accustomed to that. Frawley was an authentic and original leatherlunged jackass, and suited to his trade. After a short attempt at mourning, the mayor got down to the matter of interest.

My deeds to lots on the Cleveland side of the river to be sold at auction with proceeds donated to the Methodists

My deeds to lots on the Ohio side . . . proceeds donated to the Episcopals

My furniture and cut glass . . . proceeds donated to the Congregationalists

My wagons and livestock . . . proceeds donated to the Baptists

Impolite commentary were heard when *proceeds* from his silver and chinaware were *donated to the Catholics,* but Mr Clark had spread his bets impartially regarding on salvation. He had greased up every type of Christian. I were half surprised he had not set aside a chamberpot for the Mormons.

My home is donated to be an orphanage under the direction of Miss Sarahjoseph Fulk

My clothes to be cut up into garments for the orphans of said orphanage

This gone on and on. Poorhouse and public school and library and the militia company all come in for buttering. Mr Clark had considered everything down to his shoe buckles. As the recitation dragged, listeners murmured with boredom – cats chased after undone mourning ribbons.

My bridge at the Columbus road—

Folks sobered up instant – even tobacco spit halted in flight to hear—

—and any proceeds from its use will henceforth belong to the city of Cleveland in perpetuity

* * *

At the revelation folks looked to Mr Clark's carcass as if he might sit up in his undertaker-paint and explain. Mayor Frawley cussed some and Dog laughed his dust-laugh before screeching *TWO BRIDGES OR NONE* to the delight of certain Ohioans.

Summer.

There is a plague of rascal teachers in the west. Traveling men with no prospects and no manners and just enough hold of their figures to teach you C-A-T and D-O-G. Some come and stay for a month without spending one day sober. But even if you done all your learning in the worst shouting-school with the rascalest teacher you would see the wrong in TWO BRIDGES OR NONE. You cannot count to two without passing through one. Two makes more than none. If two bridges is preferred to none, then one bridge is halfway as good.

Unless one bridge offends your pride.

Cloe Inches did not busy herself with church-talk or promenading or temperancing. She did not indulge in anything but whiskey for digestion and to *thk thk thk thk* at a dozen dozens of tasks every day.

At the invitation of Mrs Batsab Basket, Cloe once went to the women's talking society, where they had lyceum debates as they worked at sewing. Afters Cloe dragged me behind the barn so that we could have a pipe – we hid as Mrs Tab would have ruptured to see a female use tobacco.

Cloe told me that the talking society were worse torture than whipping. *I already spent half my life sewing for s___'s sakes   You cannot tell me this were leisure*   A blue cloud wrapped her up. *I would rather listen to the boring bits of the Bible ten thousand times than another talking society*

Cloe Inches were too much of a Stiles to shirk chores, and too much herself to endure the yoke of home life. Something just burned Cloe up inside, and every so often the burning directed her outward behavior. She did not have the holiness, though she went to sermons on Sunday and knew her Bible and prayed. A trouble with Cloe were that she liked to ask questions more than is considered polite. She would lawyer you about the rightness of God's law and of the Bible lessons. We had plenty of the holiness people in Ohio, and Cloe would press them on why right were right and wrong were wrong. The holiness folks did not care too much for that.

There is appetites apart from holiness that set a person burning, but finery or flattery did not appeal much to Cloe either. I was never sure exactly what did appeal to her, apart from being left to choose for herself.

The highest consequence of Cloe's burning will were that once or twice a year she would run off from home to some other place. A country place or a city place, it did not matter. As long as it were not Ohio city. She would hop aboard an empty wagon headed home from market or talk a farm wife into sharing her horse. Or she would just walk off.

It is too much to list each escape but some notable instances:

She run off to the Shakers at North Union Pond and worked in their broom factory.

She run off to the Toledo swamp and worked at an inn on the roadside.

She rode on a canal boat to Cincinnati and seen how Germans done.

She run off to the Mormons at Kirtland.

She would not warn us before she run off, and she never sent word from wherever she gone, but she would always come back before two months were out, wearing the same frock she left in and a sheep's smile. Like she were sorry for running off and for coming back all in one. She always brung a souvenir from her travels. A cloth cap from the Shakers. A clever wooden box from the Cincinnati Germans. From the Mormons at Kirtland she had a patch of man's hair with a little bit of skin and gummy blood underneath. I did not ask how she come by that.

We never much commented on or scolded her running, the better everyone would forget it. We would all say how glad we were to have her home, and before too long she would give us a tale after dinner, before Mr Job took up the good book. The tales had amusement and wonder – Cloe could yarn – in Cincinnati she had seen a man killed by a circus elephant – the departed had been teasing the creature by yanking its ears – it were agreed by all witnesses that the animal acted justly – she said a man's mashed brains look no different from a pig's.

The story of every running-off ended the same way. After she spent her purse she would seek a position, and find herself at the same work she done at the homeplace, stooped over the same washtub or butter churn, working the same bend into her spine. She wanted some other way of using herself up, only she did not know it to say.

After her return from Kirtland we had a pipe and she shown me her Mormon scalp. There were a gray hair or two among the chestnut color. I could imagine its former owner were sore and sorry to have met Cloe.

Did they try to put you in a team of wives?

They did not try twice Out come a bush of blue smoke.

You are just like Agnes *She will not work beside another creature*

I mind other creatures less than I mind the yoke

I do not blame Cloe any. Yokes are forever going out of style. Folks bust loose for a garden of reasons – cash or kin or madness. It is an inheritance all the way back to Genesis.

If you only known this country by our decorations you would expect we had eagles falling out of every branch –

kept as pets – dined on their eggs all week and their meat on Sundays. The whole nation is tarted up with eagles – flags and banners and broadsides and news papers. Fancy furniture has even got eagles carved into it. Like Columbia did not know how to sign her name and made an eagle mark instead.

I do not know what moved the national fathers to make eagles the national creature, when we hardly to never see them. Perhaps old Philadelphia and Newyork was plagued with eagles, the sun veiled by flocks of them, the streets whitewashed with their mess. In Ohio the only eagles we seen were in the distance and making in the other direction. There were a justice to the national symbol always absconding.

Before all the bridge trouble, we crossed the Cuyahoga by ferry. For a penny old Alf Farley would float you over at Centre-street. For a penny more he would take a horse or wagon, and for another penny on top he would sell you a bag of peanuts. It were good to have the peanuts as Alf took his leisure in getting across.

By the first of June, the late Mr Clark's bridge were ready. We marked this new crossing not by peanuts but by cakes and band music and promenading back and forth. The two mayors shook hands at the center and pretended there were no bad blood between the cities. It was a fine performance but it did not keep.

Before the dawn of the second day of Mr Clark's bridge, misbehavior commenced. A sign appeared at the Ohio side.

> *TOLL FIVE CENTS.*
> *PEANUTS ONE PENNY.*

No one minded the sale of peanuts – the ruinous toll was the issue. This were five times what Alf had charged for the same number of rivers – and it was noted with sour grumbling that the bridge minder were not collecting a toll from farm wagons.

Stiles coffins had a reputation for quality that crossed the river. Mr Job did not mind the toll at all, because getting coffins across by old Alf were slow going. At our first deliveries of June, he were eager as a piglet for the bridge. Even as we approached the tolltaker's cabinet, he waved his nickel like he were eager to be shut of it.

It is twenty cents   said the voice inside the cabinet.

Mr Job pointed at the sign reading TOLL FIVE CENTS.

The voice – we never seen the tolltaker's face – said *Five for you   Five for him   Five for the ox   Five for the wagon*

Mr Job tasted his teeth some. *It is poor comedy you are asking such a price for*   This were wild impudence from Mr Job Stiles.

The voice considered this scolding a moment. *I will ask you five cents for each coffin next*

Mr Job went in his pockets for the wanting coins. *At least give us a bag of peanuts*

Asa snorted at hearing *peanuts* – they were not sugar but they would do.

It is a penny more for peanuts

Let us fly as haints again, like we did at the first hour of the year. The air is much warmer at summer, and there is no call for coat or cloak, even at the depth of night. Yet these men on the Irish town hill wear hoods over their heads. In the dark of a sliver moon their two lanterns look like unsteady eyes. These men are staggering badly. They have been keeping the company of the jug.

Ah – speak of jugs – there is Dog himself atop a mule. It is Ozias's mule Absalom – you know him by his gleaming denture. And there is Mr Ozias himself. And Mr Barzilla Fraley – a fixture of the grocery same as any stove. No surprise to see him drunk. Birt the fallen preacher. YL Honey with his new denture to rival Absalom's. Mr Philo wearing his good visiting leg, atop his fat horse Oliver. Ancient Dog and Phi carry lanterns on their mounts – how did Dog come to ride Absalom? The men on their own feet are struggling some on the lane's poor surface – they are not drunk but carrying what look like . . . barrels.

It is the first hours of the July 4 holiday now. Surely whiskey explains this promenade. There is to be a great celebration – fireworks and boat rides and dancing and cider – rastles and romance – every manner of good fun. Dog has only got them hauling whiskey down to prepare for the celebration. Perhaps they are not drunk but early to work.

You have never known Barse Fraley to be early at anything besides drinking.

Barse did not see the intelligence of hauling four firkins of gunmeal by hand. Powder is a moody substance and liable to ignite when offended. Just what were the sense in stumbling down the pighole Irish lane when a concerned party owned a half dozen wagons that might roll down the good Columbus road in style?

Barse always were generous with other folks' merchandise.

Oze!

Shhhhh

Fetch us a wagon

If you known one thing about Ozias it were that he loved his wagons and mules more than his own hide.

Philo known Oze plenty, but it did not stop him from taking up with Barse.

One of you idiots is going to spill your barrel and explode us apart   I will have two legs again but neither the ones I started with   Oze   go fetch a god damned wagon

Oze did not argue back, though he surely liked to.

*Oze   I know you hear me donkey-*lover

Oze still kept quiet, only setting down his barrel and breathing.

O—

You listen here Philo S___lips Fish—

Philo bristled to hear his name spoken so loud.

—I will not have any of my wagons exploded for a demonstration   I do not understand why we are bringing four barrels of powder if tomorrow night is only to be a demonstration   My wagons   My wagons is meant for better things than exploding—

Philo went to the eternal debate with relish. *You are missing the trick   The wagon is only to get the powder to the bridge and not paint this path with your brains if you had any OZIAS BASKET*

YL Honey whispered around his new teeth that *If you keep shouting names we will surely—*

Despite YL's good sense the lyceum kept on for some minutes, drunk preacher Birt putting in vile talk too filthy to write, Oze and Phi lashing each other like it were daytime, YL trying to make peace, Barse wishing he had said nothing at all.

Dog had kept silent on Absalom's back, but the chatter were too much to abide. *You cretins ought to let your mouths rest same as your brains   We cannot take a wagon because a wagon wants a good road   and if we take Clark's good road we will be marked   And if we are marked I will personally feed all your marital parts to my cats*

Dog swung off Absalom calm as a spider. He looked too brittle for the work, but he grabbed up Ozias's barrel and resumed the march down to the bridge.

A holiday were not a holiday without a dawn toast from Miss Dolores. She had a poor temper and were not much to look at, but on the nation's birthday our ancient cannon had a whole regiment of beaus feeding her as much breakfast as she liked.

krTTHWANNFFNG a half minute

krTTHWANNFFNG a half minute

krTTHWANNFFNG—

I will not write out the whole toast, but she mentioned each of the twenty-six states, hollering in the general direction of Washington city. Her remarks was a success as far as grabbing me out of sleep. I opened up the attic window and seen by the dawn that Big's bed were untouched. He had not been himself – man or spirit or squirrel – since his hopes of work from Mr Clark had been dashed so quick. He had spent spring and the start of summer in a low condition, seeking feats and not often finding them.

My brother owned prime lots in my mind and I worried on him. But the Fourth were not a day for fear. It were a time for cider and frolics and boat rides and joyful things. Starchier folks come together for toasts and benedictions and *Hail! Co-lum-bia's fav-o-rite son Hail! Im-mor-tal Wash-ing-*

ton. I did not mind if they hogged all that for themselves – I would take their slice of the rowdier doing.

At the front of the parade were our six aged patriots – living veterans of the great revolution. The oldest of the old were Ahaz Farly, near to ninety, clutching a musket like he were still on the watch for King George. After Ahaz came the twins Rufus and Richard Feely. Rufus were blind and Richard were deafer than bricks, but together the twins had their senses. After the Feelys went Gunt Stephens, rolled in a chair by his son, and after Gunt went Gid Gaylord, as thin as a broomstick and not nearly as personable. At the back of the regiment was Mr August Dog Dogstadter, whom you have met already. Dog had only been a servant boy during the revolution, but he wore his red-and-blue soldier suit prouder and meaner than any of the others – matched with the rusty sword from his grocery wall.

The celebration could not start until the parade reached the square, and the parade could only move as quick as the patriots. At first folks only cheered louder and waved their kerchiefs. But after a quarter hour the cheering dimmed. After Gid sat down on a stump to rest, Mayor Frawley made a suggestion that the ancient ones climb aboard a wagon to spare their feet.

The patriots did not care for this idea, and brittle old-fashioned cussing were heard. But Frawley signaled the gray-and-gold suited militia to load up the aged brigade. The privates chased the brass band off their wagon for the purpose. The Feelys was captured quick enough, and Gunt were simply lifted by his rolling chair. Gid Gaylord were hooked under the arms and dragged up. Only two fought on – ancient Ahaz swinging his musket like a club, and spry Dog waving his rusted sword and promising *lockjaw to any who breathes on me.*

The skirmish at the parade showed you what good cheer looked like on Dog Dogstadter. Nothing suited him like a celebration, and the Fourth were his very favorite. He had a surpassing love of country.

So cheerful was Dog that he submitted to a demonstration of Dr Strickland's famous new kreosote, which had done such wonders for YL Honey. Before a curious crowd the dentist painted up Dog's busted-crockery teeth with the stuff. A minute gone by and Dog did not holler – only stamped – gestured for a jug – worked his cheeks as bellows – spat blood-and-whiskey – smiled.

They were still the ugliest teeth in Ohio but they had gone from brown-green to linen white. As the crowd applauded the kreosote, Dog gave a curtsy and then went to strangle the dentist. Barse Fraley were there to grab up Dog and lead him off. As they gone, Dr S offered a last bit of advice *Only remember not to smoke any cigars or pipes today Mr Dogstadter The kreosote is liable to ignite*

* * *

After pork and beans and plum cakes and sugar-slings, we were all greased for a rousing dance to finish the Fourth. Mr Ozias offered up the yard of his barn, and all his mules watched from their stalls, our lanterns bouncing off their great brown marble eyes.

Even though Ozias and his neighbor Philo cussed each other up and down the day, they missed no chance to play music together. When they took up their fiddles – you might mistake their scraping for lovers' talk. When they sat to play, everyone in Ohio hoofed in delight.

Skirts swirling and feet flying is a catching mood. Even Mr Job and Mrs Tab had a trot. With a squint you could just see them as young folks. Myself I had put on a gingham and rubbed my hair with a candle. I felt bold enough to snap at Dot Umbstetter and chase her for a kiss – and then Mary Honey, YL's sister – and then Lucinda Butts. Between each I returned to a jug which *glunk*ed in agreement that we were having a fine time.

Phi and Oze set down their instruments only to briefly argue over the next tune. I found Miss Cloe finishing a shuffle with Elijah Frewly, the worst rastler in Ohio, who wore black eyes regular as whiskers. Cloe gave raccoon-eye Eli a bow and he went off. I gave him a nod as he gone, and made a curtsy of my own to Cloe. She laughed to see me in my manners. The sun was in bed already but Cloe had kept its light in her smile. Or the light were only the whiskey sling. I did not particularly mind which as Philo and Oze struck up "The Devil's Dream" on their fiddles.

Cloe and I hooked up our arms and twirled around happy as fools. She wore a handsome calico, black and blue and white, and stood as tall as me. Phi and Oze were just burning the place down and every instrument of my own were working too. My ears and my eyes and my skin and my nose. I felt a burden cast off and I felt sister Cloe . . . I felt something unstuck. A mote from my eye. A beam from my eye. I wondered if this were how Big seen Cloe.

An idea bit me. I felt sure that the entire world bid me to say something.

To say.

To say I did not know what.

I looked over Cloe's shoulder like the answer were in the air and I swear that one of the mules looked at me and said *Go ahead*

I did not know myself but that would not discourage me. As the fiddles stopped to catch breath, I ginned up my mouth and—

Big's voice come out.

My brother roared into the barn. I do not know where he had spent his July 4, but the absence had braced him up some. There were oceans of refreshment behind his smile, and his hair were shining worse than brass.

He grabbed up Cloe and me both and spun us around and around the barnyard, his laugh louder than one hundred fiddles.

*   *   *

With the dance over, folks climbed onto wagons, their merry hearts jingling like coinpurses. Big handed Cloe up to me but did not climb on himself. Instead he only stood with his hands on the boards like he were peering in a window. The whites of his eyes pinked at the late hour. Next to him Asa's tail swung like a scold clock.

Cloe

You could just tell from his look that he were about to trample good manners.

I busied myself with buttons on my trousers.

Tell us on the way Big   Cloe begged.

Cloe   let us be married

Big it is too small an hour for this s___   Cloe were not past public cussing at small hours.

I haven't got any fortune   but you are all I want for

I am not a want

Asa sided with Cloe in the quarrel, and started home without any *huphup*. Big watched us go, his hands still on the absent sides of the wagon.

On the night of the 4th, we have been informed, an attempt was made to explode the Columbus road bridge. Four kegs of powder were touched off under the Ohio side. No one was injured, but considerable damage were done to the timbers of the bridge. There is but one sentiment regarding such gesture. Whatever the opinions of the authorities and citizens of Ohio city regarding the bridge question, we are satisfied they would not countenance such acts, but would happily aid in ferreting out and punishing the malefactors.
—*CLEVELAND DAILY ADVERTISER*

July 5 come in with a *krTTHWANNFFNG* same as July 4, but this did not sound like Dolores. This were a younger and ruder voice. Through a head full of frogs I asked *Big have you heard that?* but his ears and the rest of him had not come home after the latest spurning.

I heard stirring soon enough – Mr Job were in the lane speaking to neighbor Mr Dennes. I run down to join them and saw a steeple of smoke climbing out of the river valley in the direction of the Columbus road.

* * *

By the time we arrived at the bridge, most of a hundred Ohio citizens were gathered to stare at the mess, with a matching crowd on the Cleveland side. The western half of the bridge had been treated awfully – half the covering blasted to splinters, some planks and posts dislodged, many more scorched. The stone legs survived, but no wagons would pass for a while. On either side of the damage, mayors Frawley and Willey patted their hands to the bridge like they was doctoring a sick animal.

After a period of consideration they marched toward each other to jaw. Just before the magistrates met, our Frawley stepped onto a busted plank and fell halfway through. Willey did his best not to laugh, but the crowd on both sides let loose. As Willey pled for decorum, Frawley went ahead and talked while stuck in the bridge.

Willey, what do you felons mean by this?

Do you suggest this is the work of Cleveland?

I do not suggest but know it

Frawley, what good would we do by exploding our own bridge?

Mayor Frawley was a curiously formed man with a long bulbous trunk and short limbs, akin to a badger or ground hog. To a person on the riverbank, gazing up at the bridge's underbelly, he must have looked like a strange cow's udder.

Despite this indignity, Frawley had no trouble talking.

If this is done by Ohio citizens, it is only the fruit of your side's chiseling

Do you mean to say you approve of this monstrous deed?

Willey, I will thank you to get your words out of my mouth Tremendous wriggling.

Frawley, let me help you out of the hole Reaching down. *Quit kicking*

After much fuss, Willey freed Frawley from the bridge's embrace. It were the last good manners between Cleveland and Ohio for a long stretch.

With half the world gathered to gawk, the morning were prime for agitating speeches. The east siders talked of a militia detachment to guard the bridge, and white-toothed Dog screeched that this militia meant to *murder us in our beds Check your straw for gunmeal before you bed down* Mr Philo only said between breakfast sips of whiskey that this madness cinched it for *two bridges*. Mr Ozias said he were surprised to agree with Phi – almost like they was acting a pantomime.

You wonder who profits when two neighbors go after each other's eyeballs in such a manner.

My consideration – the sour blood between cities were only busted romance. I once saw young John Stiles pull at the pigtails of Katie Basket, and Katie shove him into a pighole. The bridge were Cleveland yanking at Ohio city to speed a marriage. But Ohio would never consent to wed until Cleveland sat in a pighole.

*   *   *

Christ says that if a man smites you on one cheek, you ought to show him the other, so that he might smite you better a second time. If that same fellow come after your coat, you ought to hand it over, along with your cloak and your britches and your drawers too. Resist not evil et c.

Regarding smiting of faces and stealing of coats I seen what Christ meant mostly. If you are always returning such conduct the whole world will always have a sore face and a naked ass. I did sometimes wonder how matters would go if we all obliged. What becomes of the smiter? Who is this fellow clobbering and stealing shirts? What goads him to the work? Maybe he is a drunk fool – maybe he is sorehearted – maybe he only wants someone to talk at and knows no better way than to pull pigtails. Maybe he is only naked and wants a coat.

> We do not credence the insinuation of the *DAILY ADVERTISER* that the explosion was the work of *this* side of the river, for the purpose of throwing odium on the *other* side. This attempt could not be meant as a joke, unless death and destruction of property are so defined.
> —*OHIO CITY ARGUS*

On the *other* side, the money made from tolls and peanuts mended the battered bridge soon enough. On *this* side TWO

BRIDGES OR NONE became the motto, which only posed another question – was TWO or NONE better?

No one known for sure who authored the exploding. On the Cleveland side they named a dozen reasons why it must have been Ohio city, and on the Ohio side, those dozen reasons were rearranged against Cleveland – even as it were generally suspected that August Dogstadter were involved. Every piece of evidence were either proof of the other side's guilt, or proof of your side's clean hands. In Cleveland at least there was certainty that the bridge were worth protecting. In Ohio we could not decide whether we were for bridges or against them.

Mayor Frawley – after his dignity recovered from his tumble – called a meeting of Ohio city to settle whether we backed TWO BRIDGES or NONE. At the fifteenth of July, Ohio men come together at Dogstadter's grocery to see what their brains added up to. The meeting begun with Dog announcing he would stand refreshment, which put a cheer in the room. With toasts still ringing off the weapon-hung walls, Dog made another grand gesture. From nowhere he produced a firkin of gunmeal and *thrunck*ed it to a tabletop next to a flickering lard-rag lamp. A cat fled and whiskey jiggled in cups in alarm.

Dog threw a gaze around the room like he were slapping people in the face, while his lips wrestled together. Before he could let rip, Frawley pushed him toward a seat. Which took a measure of exertion despite Dog's advanced age.

During their scuffle Philo went to move the burning lamp away from the keg. As Phi clomped away, the flame seemed to reach back for the barrel like a babe for teat.

With Dog pacified, Frawley waved his short arms to hush us and went straight to matters.

Will we have TWO BRIDGES? A flap of his right arm to some sober *yeas. Or* NONE? A flap of the left to many oaths and bangings on tables.

Dog nominated himself to speak on behalf of NONE. His lawyering were admirably brief. If we could not have our own bridge, Cleveland should not have theirs. Half of the Columbus crossing were ours by right, only Mr Clark had forgot to say so in his will. If half the bridge belonged to Ohio, then Ohio had the right to half-destroy the bridge. Cleveland could do with their half how they liked.

Even with Dog speaking so bald in favor of destruction, and *thrunck*ing kegs of powder, Frawley kept up the charade that the first bombing had been the work of Cleveland. He said that he appreciated Dog's vantage but that it was *too much like the late and untoward attack by unknown felons from the east* The mayor found his taste for hot air. *In the race to be the great metropolis of the west, the victory of Ohio city is inevitable* he reasoned. *And war will only slow matters Our destiny is to overtake Cleveland And we wish it done sooner than later Only a second bridge will do*

Every table in the place come in for banging – both sides of the question were offended. The NONES bellowed dissent and the TWOS asked what money would pay for a new bridge.

I BEG YOUR PATIENCE said the badger mayor to quiet the rumpus. *You forget that we possess a natural wealth   We have got a spirit at loose ends for work*

Mr Job spoke up here on Big's behalf.   *Mayor   Big cannot work for free any longer*

Of course not   I would never suggest it

So you propose to pay him hard money for the making of a bridge?

Money of a sort

Before he run off, Carl Swarthout were a farmer. He tilled the soil and brung its fruits to market, trading for what he needed and taking the rest in paper money. He got along fine in this way until paper money went to squirrels on him. On one of his trips into town from the country Carl Swarthout went to swap shinplasters for home provisions. But the merchant pulled out a paper listing the trustworthiness of bank money, and said he would take Carl Swarthout's dollars at one-half their stated amount.

Carl Swarthout were wroth at this. He informed the merchant that he did not care for such japes. The merchant said that Carl Swarthout could keep the money and he would keep the merchandise. So Carl Swarthout choked down his wrath and paid his bill and gone back to tilling. Each time he called on a merchant, it seemed his paper money were in worse regard. Of course you cannot have a household without stuffs, so Carl Swarthout were soon deep in credit. Before too many trips Carl Swarthout were promising next year's harvest to pay yesterday's bill to get today's credit. So it only took one bad harvest to bust him wide open.

In the book of Genesis, when the fruits of Cain's fields are spurned by God, Cain kills his brother Abel as a consolation and runs off to the Land of Nod. Carl Swarthout did not have a brother to kill and did not consider that God were responsible for the trouble with the shinplasters – which are not mentioned at all in the Bible. But he went ahead and chased himself off all the same. He did not wait for any mark of sin, not wanting his creditors to find him. In honor of Carl, we made a Webster's word of his name.

To SWARTHOUT were to go fugitive and vagabond from your debts.

Big's salt had lost even more flavor in the weeks after Cloe's latest spurning on July 4. He spent his nights in a jug and his days abed.

Which is where Mayor Frawley found him the day after the grocery debate. It tickled me some to see the mayor and other dignified folks in our barn attic, making an embassy to a snoring Big. Mr Philo tickled at Big with his visiting leg and eventually one beady eye popped open. The idea of waking did not please Big and he made it known with bear-like swats at Philo.

He eventually gave in and was greeted with a proposition. Mayor Frawley dared him to consider the adoration awaiting the hero who built *a new crossing   right in the gut of the river docks   sure to carry commerce and custom*

Big said *I will get after that bridge once you learn me to make adoration into hard money*   His manners was threadbare but he made a fair point.

The mayor leaned over to whisper into the tangle of shining hair over Big's ear. Big nodded slow and said *I suppose so*   I do not know what he supposed or what Frawley proposed, but all parties shook hands.

With the embassy concluded, the day begun in earnest – I whacked away at coffins and Big wandered off. When he returned to roost that evening, he held funny flowers in a hundred colors. Shinplasters and bank papers and promissory notes by dozens, folded over as thick as a prayer book. Big went searching for Cloe to make a gift of this bouquet, but she were on errands. So he left the money in a heap on her bedding and came to fetch me.

Little brother   let us build a bridge

Big were not any carpenter like Mr Job and I. But he could swing a hammer, and with enough nails, anything will sit still. He had brains enough to look for a primer on where the nails belonged. The day after his paper money come in, he rose early and dragged me behind him on Agnes's wide back. We went down to the bridge, still singed from the bombing, the tollbooth guarded by two sheriff's men. Big hidyed them and said his intent.

We are surveying the bridge he announced.

The voice in the tollbooth said *Surveying is not allowed   This bridge belongs to the city of Cleveland*

I only want to look at the bridge   I promise I won't bust it any

Looking at the bridge on purpose is not allowed

Big considered this for a moment, then clobbered one of the sentries in the face. The other only made a curtsy with his arm as if to present the vista.

Big asked the voice in the booth if he minded.

No answer.

Give us some peanuts as well

Peanuts are a penny

After the voice had his penny and we had our peanuts, Big dug paper and coal from his shirt and shoved them into my hand. From there he commenced to swing around the bridge like a circus ape, climbing above and beside and below and hollering back what he seen.

A heap of stones around each leg   Maybe a hundred rocks the size of a good ham

Hanging from underneath by his legs with his hair falling toward the river.

Timbers one forearm wide

Standing atop the whole works.

Thirty-three Bigs long
  Five and one-half Bigs wide
    Three and one-half Bigs in height

I did my best to put all the numbers down as he called them. I would not swear that I caught every single one.

For steady weeks Big made a dervish at the site of the second bridge, hammering and sawing and splashing in the water. Mrs Tab brought him cakes and bacon so that he could keep at his tools – she would never say so but she were tickled at his useful turn. The dervishing went on until the last day of July, when Big announced his bridge ready.

Another celebration were required.

Even in the rosiest mood you could not say my brother's bridge were handsome. Big had been raised by a carpenter but he had never learned to work wood neat. His creation wore mismatched timbers all over. In some places the planks were too long, in others too short, and nowhere straight. The whole contraption seemed to have a touch of rheumatism. But by all looks, it went from one side of the Cuyahoga to the other. So you could not call it anything but a bridge.

Big would not let anyone cross until the celebration was done, so we roasted up pigs and picknicked and threw bowls and spectated at rastles. Everyone come out in their finery, even Mr Clark's dandified orphans. Big rastled Barse Fraley and flung him through both sides of a barn. We all laughed when Barse limped back, dipped in manure and feathers and smashed eggs. Asa and Agnes chased after each other like pups, and jugs seemed to empty themselves. Across the water there were a small crowd of Clevelanders gathered, puffing at pipes and watching us make merry. They did not seem angry, only curious. Back in Ohio, Big kept looking for Cloe – he wanted that she would join him in crossing first.

Mr Job and Mrs Tab and I known something Big did not, on account of his working so keen. Cloe had run off some days before. She had tied up Big's money in an old rag and left it at the attic along with a letter. Big had not found either because he had not returned home to sleep. Mr Job and Mrs Tab did not know what the letter said, but they might have imagined.

I swear I only put my nose into the letter by mistake.

> *Big.*
> *I am run off.*
> *Do not look for me.*
> *You ought to stop asking us to marry.*
> *I will not answer any different.*
> *Your sister,*
> *Cloe.*

I should have told Big right away, but he were so cheerful at his work.

* * *

The carousing around the new bridge gone past the late July dusk, and lanterns and flambos come out. But no one crossed. Big kept to his idea that he and Cloe be the first, even as patience wilted some under the late hour. It come into my mind that I ought to tell Big about Cloe – that we ought not wait for her. I found him sat among the rubbish of the great picknick meal, watching the moon climb over his bridge. In the sparse lamplight, his hair did not shine but flicker.

Cloe is run off again, Big

He wore a face like his guts had not moved in a month.

I surmised

I expect she will come around   I said without belief.

I am afraid she means it, Meed

Means what?

That she does not wish to marry   *I am afraid she is telling the truth*

I were struck to hear my brother say he were *afraid* of something. For nine years on end nothing had scared him, excepting night pigs.

After Big nursed his hurt feelings a bit longer, he went off to tell Mayor Frawley that the bridge ought to open. The mayor were much too refreshed, and gone right to hollering how we *will invade Cleveland and wag our rears under their noses!*   *We will not pay any toll to do so!*

His braggadocio galvanized the gathering. Folks grabbed

up the lamps and lights hung around the celebration and run for the bridge. From the stampede you would think that half of Ohio had bet on themselves to be first to cross. *Thuk-thukthuk* of five hundreds of shoes and hooves on timbers, and lanterns bobbing in the night like monster fireflies. What a sound and sight! You could never fit such spectacle inside a theatre.

Big and I watched from the riverbank. He did not voice pride in his creation, but only wallowed in sorrow over Cloe. I accused him of sentimentality in my mind, but allowed that he were only drunk and disappointed. Just as I forgave him, I heard a different noise from the bridge, louder than all the *thukthukthuk*s, like an empty bucket banging the insides of a well. Then a sound like pitching straw, and a general wailing. The great cloud of fireflies went down to the water and extinguished. Big's bridge had fallen.

The disaster shook Big from his melancholy. He set to the work of rescuing with an appetite. Thrashing in the dark water of the river, he grabbed up every living thing he found in the busted timbers. Before a half hour had gone, Big had swum to the wreck a dozen times and pulled to dry land every single soul that had been on his bridge. They were bruised and generally bothered but alive, all thanks to Big.

Even with the consolation of rescuing folks, failure trimmed Big's pride considerably, and he took it hard. On the morning after the disaster, I found his strawtick empty once again and his Agnes gone from the barn. And the morning after, and the morning after that, stretching into weeks. We was used to runnings-off from Cloe, and now Big had got the taste. He had authored the occasional spree before, but nothing like this summer's vanishings.

Big's failure also diminished his reputation somewhat. Kinder talk held that he were only out of practice, but there were whispers that his spirit were permanently reduced. I do not know about all that. All that were certain is that Big did not have the gift of bridge-making. Of course he has got weaknesses. We are all termited with them. But he is not ate up. He will come roaring back on you. I would bet it all day – call the wager.

You look vexed. You have got questions before you lay your bets. You would like to know what were our father and mother, how I am not a spirit, et c.

To your last: Kin comes in colors like horses. I am not troubled by our difference. I do not resent my brother his nature. A touch of envy will not spoil my love, any more than pigs eating mess spoils their ham.

I cannot story you on our father and mother who died before I had brains enough to know my sadness. The Stileses is the only parents I ever known. Big had a few years' head start on me so he known our folks a bit. He recalled them as stout and good-natured, not spirited at all. He did not say so as scorning, only as a fact.

I sense a curiosity. You wish to know where Big's spirit truly come from.

It come from fruit.

Ten years before today, before Big whomped the trees or the lake, before Cleveland had five thousand and Ohio city one thousand souls, our side of the river held barely a dozen houses – we had to cross into Cleveland on old Alf's ferry for store goods. But both sides had certain notions already fixed in their brains – foremost the idea of SPEED. Men talked of how fast the cities would grow once the canal were cut, how fast dollars would stack up. In the meantime

they satisfied themselves with races. Horse, boat, foot, anything at all you could bet on.

Summer were the prime season for derbies. Folks made
a contest of growing the largest vegetable, of the prettiest
cows and sows, but mostly of whatever one body could do
faster than another. Corn shucking and butter churning
and plowing. As children we did not have horses to race or
whiskey to drink so we made what races we could – running
– treeclimbing – swimming – rounding up shoats or roaches
and racing them. It is easy to race pigs if you have got slops.
To race a roach, by vigorous poking, is a more intellectual
manner of sport.

At summer's close, the sporting men of Cleveland
declared a great race. A purse of twenty-five dollars to the
fastest mile. All of Ohio city crowded aboard the ferry raft to
gawk at Water-street, home of the speed-way. There the fast
young men stripped down to shirtsleeves and Cossack-cut
pantaloons, drank, insulted each other, rastled, drank,
threw dice. The horses did their own preening, snorting
and stamping in the afternoon sun, wearing fanciful names
of Virgil – Meteor – Rocket – Golden Hind.

Like a cloud bursting, the *tacalatacalatacala* of thirty-two
hooves roared up and down Water-street and every heart in
the crowd *tacala*ed back. The handsome chestnut Decatur
took the stakes by three lengths. Dollars and maids' kisses
for champion Luke Lumpkin. Refreshment for everyone.

The younger brains in attendance caught fever at the
spectacle.

* * *

A week later word spread all over Cleveland and ferried across to the western village – there was to be a children's race in the middle of September, in imitation of the sporting young men. A quarter mile around the burying ground at Erie-street. Spread the word. Run however you like. On your feet or atop a spry cow, a mule, a sturdy dog, an elephant, a herd of roaches. The real cannonball news were that the winner would take a PRIZE stood by Mr Eells, whose emporium were near the graveyard.

Mr Eells were grim and sturdy, resembled to a barrel of crackers. Perhaps his always being near to barrels made folks see one in him. He would not give any twenty-five dollars or maiden's-kisses for prizes – only a barrel of apples. It does not sound like much but to a child, a barrel of apples is a fortune.

At the day of the derby, Mr Job had us help neighbor Mr Dennes to dig a latrine. As we worked, kind Mr Dennes listened to us chatter about the great race. At work's end he made a lordly gesture. He unhitched his tired dray Samantha and said we could enter her in the derby as long as we brung her home and fed her after. Samantha come to be the Lord's sewing needle. But I am in front of myself.

With the day's work done, and grown folks too tired to begrudge children their mischief, all the younglegs on the west side gathered. Myself – Big – Cloe Inches – Richard Fish, son of Philo – YL Honey – Barse Fraley – Eli Frewly, even then wearing a black eye – Job Jr, aged one. We led Samantha down to the float ferry and paid our penny fares, jabbering to Alf all the way across.

The racers that gathered were a comedy. Most run on their own feet, but Lip Wiggins rode on a winter sled dragged by three pigs. Fat Frank Dorn raced a heifer. The cow nearly grinned somehow – I have never seen a cow so keen to run. I favored our chances, though. Even worn down by years of work, old Samantha could surely outrun any cow or pig-chariot. Big would have the reins – I would take the rear seat.

Mr Eells drug the barrel of apples out to the lane. The first to circle the graveyard and touch the barrel would be the winner. With that he gave a whistle and the race were on. At first Samantha did not care to hurry. Spindly Bug Lewis and Philinda Crabtree – the fastest girl in Cleveland – darted to the front, with Cloe a dozen steps behind. At the first turn, Lip's sled struck a stone and dumped him into a spacious mudhole. Before he could stand his three pigs had joined him in the mud. At the second turn, Frank's heifer gone into the gate of the graveyard and munched at flowers. As Frank pleaded with the heifer to rejoin the race, Big finally convinced Samantha to hurry. I do not know what he whispered in her ear – that a victory would free her forever from chores – or all the apples she could eat. Whether it were truth or lies, she were convinced.

By the third turn, Big closed with Philinda, who held a hand to a stitch in her side. Only Bug and Cloe were still

ahead. I felt my heart slink down toward my guts. Samantha had worked her stubborn old bones into frenzy, and
you could see molasses creeping into Bug's twiggy legs. Cloe
kept on, even with our *tacalatacalatacala* gaining on her.

At the final stretch we pulled even – Cloe sailing with her
skirts hitched up to her armpits – workhorse Samantha and
her passengers alongside. At the very last length Big made
as a circus rider and crouched on Sam's back. Like a rastler,
he leapt forward somehow . . . and with the very last tips of
his longest fingers . . . touched the barrel of apples a foot
ahead of Cloe.

Brothers and sister and Sam and barrel all crashed
together and rolled in the dust.

Big and Cloe and I come up gasping, although I do not
know why I were short on breath.

In my mind, I felt there ought to be an entire holiday
to mark our victory. Congratulations from the cannon
Dolores. Cider and doughnuts. A parade and hours of
toasts, et c. There were no such entertainments, but pride
were enough. Big turned out to be a regular duke in sharing
our spoils. Apples for every boy and girl and living witness.
Apples for Sam, for Frank's heifer, for Lip's pigs. Apples
for Mr Eells's mules, who had no part in the race. Apples
for gathered idlers and whiskeyheads. Apples for the brave
rivals Bug, Philinda, and Cloe, who said *Let us have another
derby, Big*   with her cheeks full of fruit   *this time on your
two legs instead of Sam's four*

Big only grinned a mouthful of apples and did not brag back.

It were around then that Mr Eells hollered from inside his store that *you had better take your prize away before the night pigs come*

This is several times now I have spoken of the night pigs. I ought to give you an account.

Night pigs were just what the name suggested – pigs what went by dark. Day pigs is regular enough citizens, somewhat greedy in diet, but otherwise peaceable. Look to Lip's racers, or the late Nicholas, beloved pet of the Frewly family. Night pigs are not day pigs. Swine at liberty will turn mean faster than drunks. Your night pig is a renegado, absconded from civilization. When dark fell, regiments of these pigs come out of the woods that surrounded Ohio city and Cleveland, and ate up anything not fenced up or nailed down.

So grown folks held a healthy respect for these night pigs, who were known to eat Bibles, bedclothes, saddles, shoes, dogs and cats, et c. Children – that is to say, us – held a wilder fear of them as the very pets of the devil. Monsters what craved to eat our personal bones. Big in particular were afraid of the night pigs. In our childhood days, he never liked to be abroad too far past dark.

When the sky put on its sleeping-dress of dusk, we knew to head home. Cloe gathered up Job Jr and gone home with the rest of the Ohio delegation, but Big and I lingered on at Mr Eells's. The merchant said Big raced a horse *good as any man* and fed us a sip of his whiskey. That were enough to make Big forget the coming of dark for a moment. I did not care for how the whiskey scorched my guts, and chewed more fruit to forget the taste. The farther we dug into the barrel the tireder the apples got – I seen why Mr Eells had given them away. I were not bothered. The sweetness of victory shouted down rot.

But even on our day of glory, the sun goes down. As Mr Eells closed up his shutters, Big and I considered how to haul our prize home. A mile or more from the burying ground over to the river, down the bluff, across on the float ferry – up the other bluff on the cart path – a bit farther home. I had spent our last pennies on corn cakes besides. Perhaps Alf would let us cross on credit. And the barrel – how could we carry it on Samantha's back? What would the night pigs make of our presence?

At that thought, I swore I heard a distant sound of hogs rooting.

Now you are curious. You wonder why the famous **Big Son** would worry any at carrying one barrel of apples and rastling a few pigs.

This is the story of how Big Son come into his prodigy, so recall that he will not have any prodigy until the end.

The situation knotted further – we had been too free in rewarding Samantha. Even as we stood and considered the crisis, we had kept feeding her apples from the barrel. It is a universal fact that too much reward will spoil any creature. The more we ate, the more each apple tasted of cider. Big and I was eating near as many as Samantha and had tasted Mr Eells's whiskey besides.

The apples was drunk with rot. Without knowing, the three of us – myself my brother and Samantha – were drunk too. Factually we were good and pissed. This condition colors the rest of the occurrences.

Our fear of the pigs thickened. I gone from suspecting I heard them to imagining I smelled them. Big were convinced he saw one flash past us, lit up orange in the dusk. Samantha took to stomping in worry. I wondered if horses were against night pigs, too. Our task remained. The barrel were not worth the work of hauling, but we could not forsake our fruit. I went to Mr Eells's door hoping he might let us leave the apples overnight. But the store were shut up completely, as quiet as the graveyard across the lane. I could have sworn he had been there a moment before.

Fright grabbed at us but we did not falter – we set to using our brains.

A scheme. One brother would ride home on Samantha, while the other stood guard over the apples. This would take many hours into night – three ferry rides in all – and the pigs would surely murder the brother who stood guard. The traveling brother would have to bother Mr Job from his Bible and catch a scolding and borrow the wagon, come back east, pick up the apples and the chewed-up carcass of the other, mourn and gobble funeral fruit all the way home.

This would never do.

We set and ate more apples and rubbed together what sense we still had. I always was the more intellectual, and before too long I hit on a notion so bright as we ought to hide our eyes.

Brother   we have both got shirts and trousers

We wore shirtclothes passed down from Mr Job and mended to keep pace with our growing – too large at the front and bottom and back and everywhere.

What we ought to do is stuff our shirts into our trousers and cinch them good and tight – snug our sleeves at the wrist—

My brother were looking at me admiringly. He seen my thunderbolt coming.

—and we have only to fill up our tunics with the apples and ride home

In the dark we forged our armor. Blouses filled with ten dozen rotten apples were not the Paris fashion, but they were sewn faster and without patterns. We climbed on Samantha protected by our glory. I could feel every one of those apples on my hide – slimy and cold and grand – as I settled in behind my brother.

Big steered Sam toward the river crossing, and we was bound for safety. As we gone along we recalled the excitements of the race to each other, and reached into our shirts for refreshment. Sam could not speak but she put in her opinion anyhow, which were that she ought to have more apples. From the first steps the horse sniffed our shirts.

Soon she were expressing a curiosity about their contents. Then she chanced a bite back over a shoulder. We had a laugh at her appetite – she had eaten more apples than any of us. Sam did not consider herself greedy and kept on asking. It made for slow riding.

A second thunderbolt – we could persuade Samantha to walk straight by tossing apples ahead of us. I reached into my blouse and I chucked fruit forward over my brother's shoulder. Sam made straight for the bait, and soon we had circumstances by the tail. At the ferry, old Alf were so amused by our condition that he did not even ask for fare.

During our crossing Samantha's agitation resumed and we had no means to distract her. Samantha were clever for a drunk horse. She saw that biting did not pay and turned to bucking. Without any stirrup or rein to hold, I went flying to the timber deck of the ferry with the first kick. I struck the wood with some force but owing to the one hundred apples in my shirt I had a soft landing. It did make a considerable mess in my garments.

Before I could find my feet, Samantha had shaken Big loose. He had one foot caught in a stirrup, and his apples came tumbling out of the neck of his shirt, some splashing into the river and others rolling all over the deck timbers. Samantha snorted in joy and set to eating up the loose fruit. As she munched, my brother freed his foot and fell a short distance to the deck with a *smutch*.

You might expect we grieved our loss. We only looked at each other and Alf, and back to the brother, seen the dirt and apple stuck to our faces, and laughed into pieces. We saw how we had gone just as mad as Samantha.

Here the farce turns toward tragedy. Still shaking with laughter, we took to sport. No cannon had marked our victory so we made a salute by chucking apples. We fired them at each other as Alf cackled. Not a single apple would make it back to the homeplace. The exchange begun congenially but in the way of boys, a fool heat come into it. Before long we tried to plunk each other in the beanpot or marital parts.

The pinch come when I fired an apple toward Big Son that went over his shoulder and flush into the rear end of our horse. Sam, gone to Jerusalem on turned fruit, did not care for that. I were set to roar laughing again. But before I could draw air, Sam kicked out a back leg with mean grace and killed my brother.

Her hoof struck Big full on the side of the head. I saw the light in his eyes snuffed even as he fell – before I could reach him, blood seeped from his apple-clotted scalp.

He were dead. My good and only brother were dead for the first time.

Alf muttered *Ah s___* and I yelped in fear.

I ran to Big's side but before I could cross the short distance, before I could reach him, before any time at all, he were back on his feet somehow – no more bothered than if he had sneezed. The wound on his scalp were gory enough but only a gash. His skull held fast. I am no doctor but this was a miracle. I had seen lesser blows kill a creature.

* * *

Samantha's kick did kill Big by one thinking. It ended him as a regular person. The incident busted open some vein of lightning in his soul. Big had never been scholarly and the blow to the head did not change that any. But it put the strength and speed of fifty men into him somehow. The spirit were on him from that very moment. By six months later he were famous for his *thwock*.

You have got questions again. How did such fateful apples come to reside at Mr Eells's grocery? Did Mr Eells know the fruit were cursed? Was Sam the borrowed horse witched at all?

I have turned my mind a good deal on these matters. Mr Eells never showed any tendency toward the supernatural, before or after. "Samantha" is not the name of any sorcerer in the Bible or in stories. If Big's coming into spirit were a regular haint story, Mr Dennes would have been a stranger only passing through, such as we never seen before, and would have insisted that the orphan boys borrow his magic horse, and so on. But Mr Dennes were folks. We known him and Sam, before and after. I did keep an eye on Sam to see if she busted up anyone else. If it happened I never seen or heard. Some years later she keeled over dead as a final protest against work, and Mr Dennes had us drag her to the road. She never come back as a ghost. No, I do not consider that Sam were the trouble.

Whatever spirit touched Big were traveling in the apples, but its rupture took the mixing together of apples with the greed and glory of that night. The apples were not treated carefully, like you ought to treat a fickle substance. Gunmeal, kreosote, et c. I expect you wanted some more fanciful tale for how my brother come to his prodigy, but it were only a knock on the head. Let his accident be a lesson. We cannot live without gobbling up the world – taking its trouble into our bones and flesh – a kick will bust the trouble loose.

A confession. I am a maker of coffins but I have questions about the sense in burying.

Of course we must wait somewhere for Christ's trumpet et c. But lying in the dirt for centuries on end, all your flesh gone to feed worms, seems foolish. If Christ will raise us up in the end anyhow, what does it matter that we are buried with any particular manners? Will all our bits be mended on the great day? Will I have a new suit of clothes? Will the worms have eaten up my brain? Will they think my thoughts?

I do not say I have any better idea what to do with dead folks. Only that I hate to see such careful work hidden away.

At day time, the Ohio city graveyard at Monroe-street behaved mostly like you expect from a burying place – peaceful and lonely. But come dark, Monroe-street became the grand promenade of the night pigs. Now, a pig will go where it likes, and day pigs had liberty to wander. But after some discussion it was decided that we ought not to have pigs participating in mourning. That it were unsanitary and not entirely Christian to have swine rooting among the graves. So a subscription were taken up for a fence, and a sign posted declaring

> FIVE DOLLARS SHERIFF'S FINE FOR ANY PIG
> TO WONDER IN THESE PREMISES

I believe the sign maker meant WANDER and only spelled badly. But the mistake had a poem to it. Of course the spelling on the sign did not mean much to pigs, any more than the rest of the words or laws or five dollars. In a matter of days, the pigs had made a hole in the fence and gone back to their patch. No one bothered to rebuke them. There is not much use for a graveyard at night besides. The pigs had decency enough to leave the dead folks be.

The Sunday after Big's bridge fell, I found myself at Monroe-street without meaning to. Our mother and father were here somewhere under plain markers. In truth there were not much to remember them by, besides Big and I. We was their burying stones.

In boastful moments, Big would sometimes say his father was a wildcat and his mother was a winter blizzard.

He never said *our father our mother* Only *my father my mother*

I did not know if he set me aside as a courtesy or a cutting out.

Dusk were coming on at Monroe-street and I did not care to meet the night pigs. And there was a night-fry scheduled

– yet another congress of Ohio citizens at Dog's grocery to address the bridge question. It is when folks haven't got a good answer to a question that they ask it most.

As I walked to Dog's, the sounds of evening come in. Four-legged dogs shouting their news. Crickets at their restless prayers. Night were full with mischief, not confined to pigs and dogs and bugs. Upstanding folks bent a ways at night – romanced untowardly, raided gardens, swiped every type of creature, robbed themselves of virtue.

Not that we was all angels in white during the day. And night did have a peace – its sins tended toward quiet. As I come up to the bluff and saw the sun easing into bed out over the western water, I asked how long anger could reign over such healthy air. Even Dog's grocery looked handsome, with lamplight spilling soft from its little windows.

I found Dog at work that would be morbid in anyone else – writing his epitaph. The congress had not yet sat. Folks was trickling in and washing up their minds with drink before serious talk. Dog were seated at the back underneath his museum of violence, scratching away with a coal like he meant to ignite his scrap of paper.

In his person Dog resembled a grave somewhat – narrow at the shoulders – stooped some – worn by years. This were not his only commonplace with burying stones. Dog were always sharpening a matter down to a point, like as a marker tells the life underneath in a word or two—

MOTHER

FATHER

BELOVED CHILD

A gravestone never told how a body truly was. You never met a grave what said—

A DRUNKARD BUT KINDHEARTED AND STEADY WORKING

CLEVER AND CAPABLE BUT NEVER COME TO MUCH GOOD

WORRIED ON SIN SUCH THAT HE GOT IT IN HIS BLOOD

Dog were deep down in his sentiments. Like he believed himself pledged to a duel at dawn. He had even shaved – soap still on his cheeks – and greased his hair. You might have thought he were going courting. His sweetheart were not any woman but the fussing over the bridge.

I sat down with him and he showed me with a dash of pride the various slogans he had ginned up.

OTHERS FLED, DOG REMAINED

I WILL SEE YOU DIRECTLY

MOVE AWAY THIS GRAVE IS MINE

DO NOT TOUCH MY BELONGINGS

There was a great many more – these was only the politer ones. I considered on what other folks' burying stones might say. And my own. I were glad to stop considering when Mr

117

Job and our other friends and neighbors arrived. Not far behind were Mayor Frawley, who set right into jawing.

My friends I understand TWO BRIDGES OR NONE *I understand it to the very soles of my feet   And there is a sinew in my arm that prefers to rip Clark's bridge into ribbons   that prefers* NONE   *but my friends*   ONE *is your true course—*

Mayor Frawley had talked the bridge question so many ways that I expected his jaw might fall off – although I am not sure that would have shut him up. He might only turn about and talk from his ass. There were rude opinions circulated that he did already.

Several such rude opinions crossed the soggy grocery air.

—only it is the nature of ONE we must reconsider—

A grocery cat screeched displeasure at a tail stepped on.

—the devotion of our founding generation for the UNION—

A pork bone flew from the audience over the mayor's hat.

—we must consider whether the time has come to make TWO CITIES into ONE—

Half the room rioted. A merger of towns were a new line of talk entirely for Frawley.

D___lessness   Treason   D___less treason and a whole Webster's of profanity.

Before long an indoors thunderstorm brewed up. Hats and cats and spit and fists flown. A jug were smashed over poor YL Honey's head. The mayor hollered for *Civility   civility   We must have civility*

Ohio city were in no mood for it until   *krTTHWAN-NFFNG!*

Dog had thrown a thimble of gunmeal into his personal stove. A robe of sulfur smoke spun around him and one word came out.

NONE

Cries of approval.

Speak on it Dog   Let us hear the Dog   What is to be done?

He stepped up onto a coffin and tugged at his shirt like a preacher. One line of sweat rolled down a barber-soaped cheek.

NONE   he said again.

The assembly hollered for more but the sermon were finished.

Ohio city went to bed with Dog's *NONE* ringing in every ear. Mr Job and I rode home in a specially brown mood. The sky had opened up a warm rain that stopped any spark of chatter. Even our good ox did not give snorts and tail gestures. Under the clatter of the wagon, I could tell Mr Job were wrapped up in his particular way of silence while judging up another's foolishness. He must have been thinking on Dog's intemperance.

He never invited me inside the silence until—

Meed

Mr Job

I care greatly for you two boys and I am afraid for your brother
This were a niagara from Mr Job as far as sentiments gone.

I said Big were *heavy on my heart as well* and expected an
end of it. But Mr Job talked on at a slow trot—

*He is gone sideways   between   courting   Cloe and drink-
ing whiskey and pitying himself*

Asa brung us into the drowsy air of the barn and looked
over his great shoulder. He were listening to Mr Job's talk or
perhaps only waiting on his victuals.

Mr Job did not move to climb down. *Big has found the
slough of despond*

I climbed down and unhitched Asa as the ox minced in
anticipation of dinner.

I do not know how to help him   Mr Job said.

I spread out a dinner of hay for Asa and added a pinch
of sugar from a sack hung on the wall.

Still curled forward in the wagon seat, Mr Job eyed me up
for the first time since he started talking. He looked at me
the way he looked at wood before he went to carpentering.

*I have a notion for putting your brother right   When your
brother worked feats   Before he took poorly   He were never paid
in coin   Only in adoration*

I knew I were not meant to respond. Asa chewed happily.

*Besides   how do you value a wonder working?   You do not
think to pay for miracles*

More chewing.

The trick is   He did not say what the trick were. He only
lingered a moment longer and then bid me good night.

* * *

The next morning I climbed down from the attic and found Mr Job in the barn, waiting atop the wagon, Asa already hitched and smiling.

We have an errand

The wagon wheels murmured over lanes wet with the night's rain and Mr Job were back to saying nothing at all. At Handerson and Panderson's Mr Job *whoa*ed, hopped down, disappeared into the thicket of notions.

I sat atop the wagon and hidyed folks. Quickly Mr Job returned with a bundle of good letterwriting paper and a pot of ink.

What is our errand, Mr Job?

He shoved the merchandise into my hand.

This were all

The sun were warming up the damp world and you could feel a steam rising. On our trot home we stopped at Dog's. It were terribly early for Mr Job to take a refreshment but perhaps he only meant to crackerbarrel or fetch a jug for the homeplace. I never minded a stop at Dog's and a look at news papers.

Bring your writing paper, Meed

Mr Job pointed me to the table closest to the front door, where the cats congressed in the morning light. They did not clear out for me but only blinked, curious as I were. I picked up a fat orange tom from the coffin bench to make a seat.

121

We have paid Big Son in wonder for years   Mr Job proclaimed again.

Dog spidered over to talk, clutching a tin cup of hideous-smelling coffee.

I agreed and did not say that I had heard this point already. Instead I peered at the *ARGUS* on the table and read that *Spenser, the actor, who killed Frimbley, the impersonator of statues, in a duel, at N. Orleans, is said to have been in Texas—*

Dog grumbled that Big *ought to wonder down Clark's bridge* He gulped from his coffee. *No one asked Big to do all that* night soil   *He cannot expect payment for what he puked up by his fool nature*

One of the cats *glerck*ed up a hairball, as if prompted by Dog's talk of puke. The other cats stared at the mess, glistening in the sun, like it would speak omens at them.

August   you are right without knowing   said Mr Job. *We ought to have gotten money out of Big ourselves   He were only the fruits of nature wanting husbanding*

At the mention of moneygetting, Dog squinted some as if to say *I am listening*

We will make Big into a notion   If his feats were enough to make us wonder at him   Then they will be enough to entertain folks   They will pay good money to hear them

Mr Job were glowing some with the light behind him, same as the hairball but less slimy. He were grim sober most of the time, but I could see the boy's heart showing through now. Mr Job loved tales, even if he only read scripture. The Bible has got battles and adventures in it, after all.

We will write up Big's doings into an almanac   And add in some home truths and useful knowledge—

I saw the use of paper and ink.

—and captivating drawings of Big at his adventures And advice for emigrants to the west And advertisements for Ohio city—

It would grab folks' imaginations and their money   Dog allowed.

Mr Job sat back, satisfied with what he had spit up.

You were a bastard at heart all this time Job Stiles   Dog said. I always known I liked you

Mr Job's pride dimmed some at being cussed. *How am I a bastard?*

You profit coming and going   By Big's feats first and by selling them as stories after

The money is not for us Dog   It is for Big   As payment for his feats

The very idea of giving away the profit wracked Dog into a cough, and he cussed Mr Job further. But after the contempt passed he agreed that the notion were sound – even if the money would be wasted on a fool such as my brother.

I did not think to ask Mr Job how money would help Big, if Big never came home to find it.

Mr Job never meant to carpenter the almanac himself. He left me behind at Dog's to begin the work straightaway. The fever season of summer were near to over, which meant less call for coffins. Besides, I were the natural choice for almanac-making – I knew Big best and had a good hold of my letters.

So in the warm rump of August I set up a writing factory at Dog's at the table by the windows, sat on a coffin I might have made myself. As I worked, Dog's cats licked themselves and fought, sending fur floating into the sunlight.

You cannot have a fire without wood. You cannot have a harvest without plantings. So Mr Job spread the word as he delivered coffins by himself. Everywhere he gone he asked after stories of Big and even took out a notice in the *ARGUS*.

You already know some of Big's ripest doings. There were many more I have not shown you, and folks brung in feats I had never before heard a word of. Wild garments stitched from every thread of truth and lies and fever – a hundred different Big Sons and tales of Ohio. Every person I ever met came and told on Big, and even folks I never met before came in with a piece of my brother.

The first to call were the regulars of the grocery, the drunk owls who sat and watched passings-by all day. I got about what you expect from such fools.

They had seen Big *rastle rivers and break lakes and rescue women in woe*
  Meet the devil twice and whip him three times
  Teach alligators to waltz
  Get bit by one thousand rattlesnakes and live and bite each one back
  Ride elephants as race horses
  Race against a steamboat just by swimming
  Tie together the tails of every creature in the wildness   Wild cats and wolves and squirrels and wolverines what hardly have a tail at all   Knotted them up into a monstrosity   Rode the thing to Texas and fought at the Alamo   Ate twenty-five Mexicans and escaped alive   That were Alvarado Farley, who were stuck some on the stories of Texas.
  Ate eagle eggs for breakfast and bear bacon at supper
  Taught wolves to wail
  Put the face on the moon with a rusted musket

*Pummeled one hundred rotten Clevelanders   Stole all their teeth and made a gift to Dr Strickland   That were YL Honey, still proud of his incorruptible teeth. As he storied on Big, YL took his denture out and set it on the table like a fine pocket watch.

As more respectable folks come in, the stories prettied some. They still told as much on their teller as on Big.

The government at Washington sent five millions of dollars to dig the canal and Big Son were seen to eat it up and fart out a thousand Irishmen to do the digging   And every so often you will see him cough up a dollar coin and praise for the pope   He only says he is poorly to hide the crime   That were Ozias, who always suspected Catholics and theft.

Gathered up all the liquor in Ohio —that were Philo. I wondered if he were taking the water pledge— *and switched the Cuyahoga from water to whiskey so folks could drink just like hogs*   He were not taking any pledge.

BUILT A HOUSE OF CRYSTAL FOR MISS CLOE AND HIM TO LIVE IN BUT A JEALOUS WIND BLEW IT DOWN AND STUCK HIM ALL OVER WITH SLIVERS   AND THAT IS HOW THE SHINE GOT INTO HIS HAIR— that were Handerson, before Panderson took over   *—AND YOU COULD GET THE SAME SHINE BUT NONE OF THE STICKING WITH THE LATEST NEWYORK LINIMENTS FOR PURCHASE AT—*

The finish of August and half of September vanished this way. There were surprises in who had a tale to tell, even those who would never set foot in Dog's.

One morning when I were climbing down from the attic with my papers, Mrs Tabitha ambuscaded me with cakes. As I chewed she gave her tale. *Foreswore causing trouble and learned his chores and did all the work of every woman in Ohio for a hundred years*

Not all the stories were so moral.

Woke up the dead under Monroe-street and had them dance a reel

Ripped up all of Cleveland and set it wondering on the lake as an island

Climbed to heaven and dared Christ to a rastle

Gave birth to his own child   That were Birt the soiled preacher.

Made a great balloon lifted by buzzards and vanished into the night stars

As the stories piled up and Big remained vanished, more of the tales seen him whipped or dead altogether.

Crept to Cloe's window and sung songs of devotion   But Mrs Tabitha took fright that he were a madman or a howling wolf and shot him   And that is how his heart come to break

Made a speech so tender that the millennium come down and folks had to beg to the Lord that it were not time yet

Made a ladder two miles tall to learn what a cloud were made of   Only that ladder busted and he fell forever   Hollering the whole way that he were not sorry to die only sorry he could not die a thousand times more

Took insult from the first steam engine   Said he could work as good and drank boiled water which cooked him to dying

The survivors of the trees Big chopped came for him and said

<u>Give us back the planks what you busted out of our cousins</u>   *Big said he* <u>could not give back the planks as they was the very bones of Ohio now</u>   *When next he slept the trees reached their longest branch into the barn attic and stole his bones as revenge and he woke up as a rug of skin*

Were eaten by moschitos entirely and the man you seen is actually a cloud of them in a suit of clothes

Put temperance on Ohio by drinking up all the whiskey in the west—   This were not Philo but his wife, Annabel   *—and his guts rebelled at careless thirst and his mind turned to pudding*

Said his hide were iron brewed from the very blood and flesh of the republic   And dared men to throw axes and stones at him   and so died

Gone after Hillibert and his gang of counterfeiters   Were murdered by the bandits   Who sent back a shinplaster Big Son   We never known the difference

One afternoon as I scribbled, Dog came up next to me in his silent way of moving.

I have got one for you   A tale for your almanac   A true tale
About Big?
About General Washington

There were no greater American than General Washington. His doings were fashioned into instructions for right conduct by Parson Weems and a dozen other accounts. How he would never tell a lie, et c. The almanac would not suffer with a bit of Washington.

Dog poked me in the shoulder and said that he had *seen Washington once   The living man when I were only a tadpole*

I were eager to hear how Dog would cuss Washington – he were too much praised. Dog were born to cuss – his tongue could kill a bird right out of the air.

But his talk of Washington were nearly solemn.

Dog said that the aged general were considerable swollen in his ankles and feet such that his boots were cut open at the sides. That the great man smelled of mildew. That he rode out to review the militia armies without his teeth in. That his soldiering talk come through wilted lips. That his eyes had a soaped look. That he trembled some. Dog said he had seen right there that day how *birthing a country left you ill used as birthing a dozen babes   I should never like to be a spirit at all*

I asked whether   *it were worth being used up if it made for moral stories*

I would rather be Dog alive and never storied than any dead president   Still stinking through all the flowers heaped on his burying box

I made no answer.

Will you put all that in your almanac?

It is not the popular opinion

You might put that it is the view of August Dogstadter of Pearl-street, Ohio city   Purveyor of refreshments   And I will gladly answer complaints

*

129

Folks brought me enough tales for an almanac and an *Arabian Nights* besides. Now I had to carpenter them together. I considered whether I ought to put the mostly true ones together in one heap, the less true in another, the not-at-all true in a third, the wildest ones in a fourth. Perhaps better to mix them all together, like a quilt.

Big had been absent since his bridge fell on the last day of July – a month and a half. He had left behind his red neckcloth and the hank of paper money and the letter that Cloe had left him. I sometimes thought I saw his souvenirs move around some between morning and night. But if he were sneaking back I never heard or saw or smelled him.

The nature of the work made me feel him keenly though. Like he were right there next to me adding his own bits to the tales and occasionally scattering the cats with a brass laugh. Even as I imagined Big next to me, I knew there were something missing from the hundred Big Sons I had written down.

Big did not simply wake up of a morning and know where to find feats. Folks put ideas in his ear. Sometimes it was a dire crisis and others it were only a chore someone wanted done. He would take up after anything at all. Runoff milch cows. Wells run dry. Wagons stuck in mud. Harvest hands needed. Graves wanting digging.

There were only one feat Big would not get after.

You might guess which.

Recall the night Samantha kicked Big in the head, and what were on his drunk brains at the moment of fate. Consider the last fright to cross Big's mind before coming into his spirit. That the night pigs would catch us and eat us.

This fear told somewhat. If you mentioned the nuisance of the night pigs to Big Son he would take up a new topic of talk quick as he could. He would chatter on town gossip or horse races or Vanburen or the price of corn – matters he had no care for – only to get you to forget the pigs.

I confess I teased him some on this account.

Big you would die of fright if the night pigs come for you
or
You would climb a tree and chop it down underneath you
or
You would run to the top of Pike's peak to watch in every direction for the pigs
or
You would run off just like Cloe

His reply varied with his mood. He might toss me up a tree. Or only tease back quiet *It were your poor aim that got me kicked in the head*

But his fear were real. He could not keep it hid under clobbering or a ready joke or Vanburen. I minded him whenever the pigs was spoken of and marked how he went tight all over. His whole person cinched up like he wished to disappear.

Once when I were needling him on the matter of swine, he let out a confession. He believed that his spiritedness owed somehow to the night pigs. That if he were to *bust the pigs up it would bust me up too*

I did not know just what he meant, but allowed this were nothing to wish for.

I sometimes thought on how Samantha might have kicked me instead of Big on our raft ride home. Or how Cloe might have won the race and the apples, if Big had not had the advantage of a Samantha. Would the apples have done their sorcery some other way?

If I were a spirit, how would I go? Would my hair shine? Who would write my tales?

If Cloe were a spirit, who could court her?

These thoughts pinched like small shoes and made poor traveling. But I could not leave them alone. I did sometimes want to possess his spirit, just once. That I might mind the difference between us less. I do not mean TWO BIGS OR NONE   Only that sometimes I thought I might like to have a feat of my own.

Big were not the only absence at the Stiles homeplace. Miss Cloe Inches remained run off since the last days of July. I would like to amend the record somewhat regarding Cloe. It is true that she were given to running off, but she were just as given to running back. She did not have a monopoly on flight. In truth, running off were something of a catching disease in the western country, and Cloe were admirable in that she bothered to return. Folks absconded for every cause you could think of. Bankruptcy and shame and ruptures. There was a whole dictionary of reasons for flight.

To ABSQUATULATE were the scientific term for departing with haste.

You already learned what it meant to SWARTHOUT.

To SPURGEON were to run off from obligations of family. After Hiram Spurgeon, the blacksmith, who had quit his kin after he had ten daughters and no sons.

To STRANG were to run off from your own wedding, a type of special SPURGEONing. After Miss Sarabeth Strang, the maid.

Sometimes we liked to say that *the night pigs had eaten* the vanished party. *She is with the pigs now*   or   *You will want to ask the pigs about him*

Cloe rastled some in her heart about what we owe each other. I had that straight from her. Once as we sneaked a smoke behind the barn she had talked on the golden rule from the Bible, of doing on others as you would be done on.

Meed if someone does poorly on me I should still act kindly on them?

That is how I take it to mean

But the swap is poor for me

I allowed she had a point but that we were not to see it as a swap, only you had to *let evil chew you up as much as it likes and not bite back*

Cloe stared at the planks of the barn side. *What about the other conduct that chews us? What if I would prefer you to leave me alone but you would prefer to drown me in foolishness? What if folks come around slapping work out of my hands and trying to marry me up?*

I had a notion which folk she meant.

If I would prefer to be left alone   and so I left you alone   And you paid me back different I am not to mind   The whole rule is brambled

I wondered if she meant more than Big's courting. If she meant the whole world to leave her be.

The wisdom of *Do unto others* puzzled Cloe. But Dog were not stumped at all. If folks sinned on you, pay them back double. If you only suspected folks had sinned on you, pay them back without asking. It is good manners.

He had no wish to swarthout on what he seen as his debt to Cleveland.

Dog never admitted he done the first bombing of Clark's bridge, but said that it were only meant as a *demonstration*. Not meant to destroy the bridge, only to scorch it some. To show Cleveland that Ohio city's grievances were serious. And besides, *are you sure* he would ask *that the bombing were not the work of Clevelanders dressed up as Ohioans to paint us guilty?*

He were lying on top of lies. I believe he had always meant to blow the bridge apart. He only regretted that he should have used more powder.

Dog had silent friends in Ohio city. I suspected Handerson and Panderson for their business suffered from the bridge. Barse and Eli must have did some of the work, as Dog were too old for all of it. Ozias come in for suspicion as well. He were sore at paying tolls to do his teamstering.

In the night between the 15th and 16th of September, under a chilled rain, Dog put a wagon full of whiskey under gum blankets. He climbed aboard the borrowed cart and drove right down to the bridge. The sentries was alarmed to see the notorious Dog. But surely a bomber could not be so brazen. Who would pay the toll to cross a bridge they meant to explode?

Dog handed down a gift to the sentries before he gone across. A jug *to keep out the damp for you boys.*

The sentries gave Dog their compliments and turned their concerns to the jug. Dog rolled the wagon across the wet timbers. There were no guards minding the Cleveland side – only the moon behind rainclouds.

During the night of the 15th, unknown parties attempted a second exploding of the bridge connecting this city with the City of Ohio. As a result of these ineffectual depredations, women and children were compelled to flee their beds in dead of night; a stone of the supposed weight of 200 pounds was forced into a neighbor's house of ten rods' distance, and the lives of families and individuals jeopardized.

Mayor Willey has ordered that the city Marshal and his Deputies keep a sufficient armed guard at said bridge to protect the same from added injury, until further ordered by the council—that the Sheriff of Cuyahoga county, and all peace officers, and all good citizens be invited to aid in the preservation of said bridge, and in ensuring the safety and lives of individuals.

—*CLEVELAND DAILY ADVERTISER*

I am regretful said Dog.

He were reading over the *ADVERTISER* account of the second bombing. He did not regret the lives of families and individuals jeopardized any. Only that this second bite had not got the apple.

I should have waited out the weather

He gone on regretting.   *Placing the powder right up next to the stones   muffles the violence some   Like a pillow   A point to remember*   he said, almost tender.

*

My green thought – that I wanted a feat of my own – stayed cinched up. I kept after the work of writing about my brother. Mr Job said he hoped to have the almanac printed not too far into October, to sell as entertainment for the coming winter.

So I would have to speed some. I sat there with my imagined Big next to me, asking him what he thunk of the various tales – how he would embroider them – which he would cut out – whether he preferred a certain feat tamped down and mostly honest – or would he have more stretchers?

Big had practice in telling lies on himself.

I recall a day several years prior when he come home with his face scratched all over, his hair full of leaves and sticks, his blouse all tatters, his neckerchief spun around with the knot at the back. Folks gawked to know who had abused Big so.

Big Son announced that he had *met a gang of one hundred man-sized weasels in the woods   And heard that they was plotting to secede from the republic and start their own nation   And he went right after them and smashed up their plots   But only after a keen fight   Biting and clobbering and every kind of rastle   But what a good scrap   Worth the death of a good shirt!*   Then a peculiar laugh.

Up in the attic that evening Big told me the truth. As he washed out his cuts, he swore me to the utmost confidence. Which I am busting only now. He had not met any hundred weasels or even one weasel. Out on a ride with Agnes he had been spooked by a sudden flight of doves and fallen down a bramble. Then he made the matter worse by flailing, and by the time he got free he had bloodied himself and ripped his blouse to ribbons.

Handerson and Panderson and every other emporium had been touting readymade Newyork shirts all summer. This were a new idea entirely – a shirt not stitched at home but for sale like fruit or medicine. One morning at the grocery the debating society took up these readymade shirts.

Barse said he would like to get himself such a shirt. He could dispense with mending or washing off messes. Only put on a fresh one every month. Eli said a month of Barse's stink would wear five shirts out. Barse cussed Eli some. Dog put in that readymade shirts was for fools and that you could trust a shirt made by a wife or neighbor but *a shirt from Newyork is liable to go bust same as a bank*   I had never before known Dog to have views on shirts but he liked an argument.

That put me in the mind of Big and his famous weasels. I could just picture him there in that ruined blouse. I asked him what he thought of Newyork shirts.

I were startled when he spoke back out loud.

His reply were not eloquence. I heard bits of cussing and lamentation in his speech but altogether it did not add up to meaning. His aspect were wretched all over. He seemed to have fallen into a porridge and let it dry on, and then lost a dozen rastles for dessert. His eyes were pink as puppies and his shirt were only a row of buttons hanging from the collar.

Flies buzzed from out of his snuffed hair and there were a hundred cuts all over his person. He smelled unchristian.

Before I knew what to think, Mr Job *shonk*ed a jug on the table beside us.

His Agnes rode up the Detroit road just now with this sorry article asleep on her back

Once Big had been baptized several times in the horse trough and doctored with refreshments he come out with an accounting for his absence—

I were swimming in the lake and took distraction and all of a sudden I had swum all the way to Canada   I thought it is time America invaded anyway   And I met with Joe Mufferaw there   he is a fine spirit up north   and we got to drinking and fooling   We were smashing maple trees over each other's heads to get at the syrup inside—

Mr Job had on his cloak of doubt in the utmost.

—and I had a cup too much drink and went looking for a place to sleep   I found a dry cave that suited   I were sticky all over with the syrup   I woke up to a dozen cub bears licking at my hide   I took startled   The cubs turned ferocious when they thought their sugar meant to abscond   And I hollered at their little sharp teeth – which woke up the mother bear   and I come in for an awful chastening from her as well   The next I knowed I were here

With the tale concluded Big put his head down and tumbled back into a wretched sleep.

Not even the worst fool in the grocery believed a word of

what Big had said. He had been absent for six weeks. Such a saga as he told were a week's doing at the most.

I wished I could ask Agnes for the truth. But I put Big's version down in the almanac anyhow.

Mr Job and I loaded Big into the coffin-wagon and brought him home, with Agnes prancing behind in worry. At the homeplace Mrs Tabitha tidied Big up as best she could – washed his wounds and combed the knots out of his hair. He had no clothes to wear after we burned his soiled rags, so we wrapped him in blankets and Mr Job and I worked together to lift him up to the attic.

Big slept for three days laid out on end. I worried over him a considerable deal. I worried whether he would ever wake, and what awaited when he did. He were still snoring thunder when I climbed up to the attic on the third night. It should have been a comfort to simply know where my brother was after his long absence. But I did not rest easy once I bedded down. In fact I itched all over, like there was wood from whittling gotten into my drawers.

I decided then that I knew the origins of my discomfort. I had always lived in the shadow of Big and I had grown accustomed to the cold. I had made small rebellions. Perhaps you guessed that I wrote down the measurements wrong for Big's bridge. I confess it. Now, after a season spent on the almanac, without Big's company but still in his shadow, I were too jealous for such petty revolts.

I were absent from my almanac, from my own life. I had

written down a hundred and one stories of my brother and not a single one about myself. I would make my mark, such that folks would have to remember Mr Medium Son.

Only one feat would do.

I would do what my brother could not. I would chase the night pigs out of Ohio.

I could taste the praise. Folks would say *We have a second spirit   O ho what a wonder!*

How would I go about it? My mind sawed away, same as Big's *brrrghhg*.

How does a person do miracles?

It is not science but a work of sentiment. Simplest is best. How would Big have done it – if he were not scared so bad of pigs? Thrown them all into a sack – hopped in and pummeled every last one into good behavior or bacon. I turned and tugged and put some brain grease to the knot, and finally it come undone. It were not a question of how *Big* liked to do – but how a *night pig* liked to do.

I known pigs here and there – how they acted and how they tasted to eat. But the only pig I were ever on personal terms with were Nicholas, who lived in the mudhole behind the Frewly homeplace. Nicholas were beloved – always making his manners around town – visiting for a scratch behind his folded ears – a smile in his eyes. He were more a four-legged dog than pig.

I recall when the Frewlys finally ate Nicholas and how they invited folks for the barbecue – how we all shared fond memories of the departed even as his head sat on the table – the smile in his eyes not entirely gone.

What I remember of Nicholas apart from his good manner and good meat were that he were awful easy to fright. A loud startle, even an axe *thwink* or hammer *churrk* at a surprise moment, would set him to running with a *skweeent* and you might not see him for days.

At the very deepest part of night, I crept out under the snores of my brother and snuck into the homeplace. Going like mice, I borrowed Mrs Tab's rubbish pail full of bones and rotten vegetables. Back in the yard I seasoned the rubbish with all manner of filth – crap from the animals – corncobs from the privy house – I thrown a few eggs in as well. The stink of the bucket were thick enough to float a duck. Before I marched off I gathered up some cakes and my pipe and some lucifer matches, and stowed them inside my shirt.

So armed, I took to the silent lanes. A lamp glowed here and there, but no one minded me save for the curious moon. He followed me all the way to Monroe-street graveyard, the home of wondering pigs.

Even with the moon for company the burying yard were fearful lonely. My fright does not need apology. I do not see you visiting any graveyards at the rear cleft of night. The work put some whalebone in me. Even if my courage failed, the smell of the terrible bucket might have kept me brave. I went under the branches of the oak trees at the center of the graveyard, where the moonlight come through as freckles.

At the foot of one burly tree I poured out the bucket of filth in a neat puddle. With the banquet served I shimmied up the trunk and sat myself on a sturdy sidelong branch. It were a fine night – cool and dry – owls hooting and crickets fiddling. In the peaceful air the thrill of my adventure flickered some with waiting for the pigs. So I made myself a pipe to pass time and drown out the stink. It took nearly all my lucifers to get a smoke going.

About as soon as I were enjoying my pipe I heard stirring from the Umbstetter place across the lane. A door thrown open – slow footsteps. This corner of the city were thick with Pennsylvania Germans come west. Somehow despite my stealth Mr Umbstetter had seen me. Perhaps his German nose were keen for tobacco. Or he had marked the *snikpf* and flash of lucifers. Or I were not as quiet as I thunk.

Halloa   halloa

Mr Umbstetter had not featured in my plan. This seemed a step sideways.

You   in tsee baum

I squiggled some and acorns fell.

Yes   I tsee you

Mr Umbstetter marched to my tree. He were clutching a lantern up to his face, near enough to toast his whiskers. I tried to make a statue of myself but it were no use.

Hidy Mr U

Herr Meed?

No polite talk came ready to mind.

Ya   halloa   You are in tse baum for why?

As I looked for a reply Mr U creased his nose at the smell of the pig-lure.

I   were   paying respects to my folks

Even as I spoke I known the lie were a poor one. The departed should not be used in deceit. And you do not need to climb a tree to mourn. And mourning is typically done in daytime. And the filth et c.

Ya   ya Mr U were respectful but you could see the doubt in his mind.   Finally he determined it were not worth the lost sleep.   *Gute nacht Herr Meed   Careful of tse schwein*

The evening swallowed me back up after Mr U gone. No one there to laugh at my fool self but I still felt pricked all over. A bit of time passed before I were cured of the embarrassment. That pause were enough for fear to catch up with me. All night I had run on my desire for a feat of my own – never stopping to mind any fright at battling the pigs – finally I had slowed some and my coward shadow had grabbed my ankles.

It were just as well – fear were the very thing – I have not told you the workings of my scheme.

Recall Nicholas and how easy he took fright. A sudden startle and you would not see him for hours. My idea were that night pigs shared the same family trait as Nicholas. If

I put a bad enough scare into them they would leave Ohio entirely.

That is the entire scheme.

But the workings had an elegance. The scent of the bucket would call them to supper, and as they ate I would come screeching down out of the tree like the worst owl – a ghoul mad for pork. There is nothing worse than a ruined supper. Such a fright dropping from the sky would ruin a dozen suppers. I would keep at it every night. The terror I fed them would catch like hog cholera. Before long Ohio would have only mild day pigs.

Before I could put the fear on pigs, I had to survive it in myself. As the night crawled along and I wondered when the pigs would come, I could feel a fright burrowing into my very bones. I talked back to myself with a sermon. *There is no such thing as fright   It is a trick of our brains to keep folks from foolishness   To keep them from doing feats   To keep down the population of spirits*

I had never thunk on the question of spirit so. To be a spirit you cannot balk at fears. You cannot mark them at all. You must be illiterate – or even deaf dumb and blind. To be a Big Son you must get bitten up by bears without dreading it. To be a Big Son you must not mind.

I have never been bitten by bears but I have been bitten by ants and I will say that my present fear felt more like ants. You would think that fear would chew from inside to

145

outside, working out from my guts and brains toward the skin. But the fear I felt were eating at my hide. Right then I remembered my picknick cakes – not because I were hungry but because an ant crawled into my mouth.

I realized that ants were asking after me the same as Mr U. They was put out at my trespass in their tree and also curious of the cakes what I had stuffed in my shirt. Ants do not get cakes often and in their excitement they was chewing me up too. So I went to scratching modestly, so as not to give myself away. But the biting only got worse and before five minutes passed I were squirming and scratching and kicking as best I could with one arm still holding me to the tree. Agony and irony – I had thunk to ruin the pigs' dinner and now I were become a dinner myself.

You are saying *What a jack ass   Serves you*

Keep your peace. You will have more delight.

It turned out that the ants shared their tree just as Cleveland and Ohio shared the Cuyahoga. Their rival and neighbor were an owl, who objected considerably to my visiting. Just as soon as Mr Owl come home, he went right after me with his long fingernails.

This were too much to bear – with my legs kicking and one arm battling the ants, I swatted at my inhospitable host.

Count up my appendages and you will see I had forgotten to hold on to the branch.

Down we went – owl, ants, Meed and whatever else.

In my brief flight I had a lucifer *snikpf* in my brains. All my fears had drowned each other. Whatever come next could not be worse than what I already felt.

What come next were landing in the puddle of s___ spread out for the night pigs. I settled face-first with a *splurch*, and quickly the owl were gone and the ants were gone, like they wanted no part of my indignity.

Which were the least of my misfortunes. I were now alone, at night, and dressed up in what night pigs like to eat, in a place much favored by night pigs. But I did not feel any great fear. I had gone right past fear. Courage is an imbecile.

Which were good, because the pigs had arrived.

If you asked me to imagine the night pigs I would have seen them as the very devil's companions – long bristled hairs – blood-hued eyes – wild teeth as corkscrewed as their tails – and the smell! I would have imagined a stink worse than any barnyard filth – the very smell of freedom – the freedom of death – the freedom of a rotting thing.

I learned different in the graveyard that night. Night pigs was only pigs. Sleeker than day pigs what got more regular dinners – but still pigs. They looked blue instead of pink but that were only the moon's paint.

A shoat come right up to me and licked s___ from the side of my face. Her snoutbristles tickled my ear some. I dug a corncake from my blouse and offered it up as a gift. The shoat ate from my hand meek as a lamb and ran off with a cheerful grunt.

With the blue pigs circling my puddle of mess, I set and

waited for spiritedness to come over me, for something inside me to bust – like this idiocy were my Samantha-ing, my coming into powers. But my spirit did not come with any haste. Did not come at all.

I drank down a gulp of autumn air and looked through my brains for what I ought to do.

I could scream and holler and chase the pigs off – then tell stories on myself. *I battled the awful night pigs!*

I could walk home and wash off the mess and never say a word.

I could stay here among the tombs like the Gadarene – swear off britches and pretend I were a pig – wear my madness as chains.

Or I could go down to the river – wait for dawn and the first boat bound for anywhere and run off. Folks could say *The pigs took Meed* or that I had swarthout-ed for reasons unknown.

I climbed out of the filth and walked calm as Sunday into Monroe-street.

What a sight I was – though only dark windows and water puddles seen me. Somehow my reflection told me that I should go down to the Cuyahoga and wash myself.

At the crown of the bluff I seen the first breath of dawn on the eastern sky. Down along the tangled river, Mr Clark's bridge looked orange – half pink dawn and half blue night. My soiled clothes were chilling me and I shed them. There was no one to mind my jaybirding, and the air were a vigorous refreshment.

I followed the Detroit road down to Centre-street, where the timbers of Big's failed bridge were heaped on the side of the river like hay for some great creature. I walked past the steam furnace and the rope walk and barrels and boxes and bales heaped up at the canal docks – the sun peeking shy over the warehouses of Cleveland.

I came through the last of the heaps and hills of merchandise to the water's edge, eager to hear what the water would tell me. It told me that I were not alone. A long low canal packet were unloading – surly mules yawning – burly boatmen handing ashore parcels and passengers.

Among them were Miss Cloe Inches.

Next to Cloe were a man dressed all in white duck – his garments looking orange in the dawn, same as the bridge. The limbs inside the white suit were lean and long, and framing his visage were a black silk cravat and a new straw hat. The face between were crimped all over with pox scars, but somehow more handsome for it, like cut glass.

Autumn.

My joy at Cloe's return caused me to forget that I were entirely naked. I called out a hulloa and she looked right at me.

MEED! Turning sideways to escape my shame. There were rebuke in her eyes but half a grin on her lips too. *How the fashion has changed since I've been gone*

I were stuck for manners so I only put hands over my nuptial bits for etiquette.

The man with the cut-glass face stood by smiling. Behind him a boatman were piling up bags and trunks. I could not say if the man in white grinned from embarrassment or amusement or if his face just sat that way – that he and the world shared a private comedy. In all cases he did not seem to mind my nakedness any more than you would mind a breeze.

Miss Inches   Will you meet me to your friend?

Still turned sideways, Cloe chopped at the air, graceful

and surly. There was no smile in her voice as she made manners.

Meed   this is Mr Tod who were on the packet

The new man lifted his hat over his head.   *Tom to my friends and we   are   friends now Miss Inches*

Cloe did not say whether they were friends only that *Mr Tod this is Mr Meed Stiles my brother*

He stepped forward and lifted his hat even higher. *Mr Need, is it?* he asked.

Meed   with an M

He nodded uncertainly and pushed his hat higher again.

I did not have a hat to doff so I took a hand from my crotch and stuck it out for a shake. Unfortunately the hand were covered in pig mess.

Mr Tom Tod apprehended my soiled hand some before returning his own. I credit his character for being game. After we shook he held his right hand out from his body, like he would have it cut off once an axe were found.

As we made manners the boatman piled up the newcomer's possessions. This Tom Tod had brung an entire personal circus of hatboxes and carpetbags and luggage. With his clean hand Tom reached into a pocket and fished out a quarter-eagle coin for the boatman.

Take my things to the Franklin House on Pearl-street

I am not a busybody. I do not like to count other folks' money. But a quarter eagle were nearly a week's wages. The porter took the coin like it were the very host, and

Tom Tod went right back into his pocket. He fished out what looked to be a banknote and used it as a napkin on his soiled hand.

Permit me to see you home, Miss Inches   *or Cloe if I may be bold*

You may not   *My brother will fetch me home, Mr Tod*   Cloe said.   *I wish you good fortune*

I could find no better fortune than your company   He tossed the soiled shinplaster to the ground.

I thank you but surely you must look to your affairs   *Good day*

I would be a rascal if I did not escort you

The boatman edged up behind Tom Tod and collected the filthy money.

Lips pursed at the new arrival's manners. *Do what you like, Mr Tod*   *I cannot hobble you*

Cloe kindly gave me her shawl and I covered up. It were good of her – I do not know how Adam and Eve kept their fig leaves in place. Meanwhile this Tom Tod returned to his pockets again and come out with a bottle of scented water to pour on his hands.

As he rubbed on an improved smell, Tom asked me *What kind of a name is Meed?*

Short for Medium

And what kind of name is Medium?

Before I could say what kind, Tom Tod announced he could *just taste the prospects in this place*   *The west is ripe*   *The Lord's own garden for money getting*

He liked to pose a question but did not seem to mind how folks answered. Miss Cloe had bolted ahead already and we went to a quick step. As we trotted Tom were always diving back into his pockets for some notion or another. First it were a pocket watch – then it were a cigar to bite between his teeth – then it were lucifer sticks for *snikpf*, setting the cigar burning.

Mixed in with the brisk pace and the pocket fishing and the cigar puffing he ran his mouth too.

On my travels I have seen pastures and purple valleys   A country singing out for the plow   For the factory   For progress etsetra

I did not know how to reply – I did not know what travels he meant – it were hard in any condition to make conversation hurrying uphill in a diaper.

I have seen riches just asking for hunting   Like pigeons   All a man has to do is shoot

I had never known gold eagles to drop easy as pigeons.

And what feathered fortune do you stalk Mr Medium Stiles   Apart from a suit of clothes?

Skilled as he were with hands and mouth Tom Tod did not bother much with ears. Even as I mumbled a reply I noticed his eyes pointed at Cloe up the hill.

From his stall Asa seen Cloe into the yard and he went to hopping with gladness. The whole homeplace soon joined – the seven young Stileses run out in their bedclothes to hug Cloe's skirts. She had run off and returned before, but never for two months. The children had not seen their Cloe from the middle of July 'til this first day of autumn. A bit of sentiment come into the corner of her eyes at the embrace of the little ones.

From inside the barn I heard the sound of coffin-sawing pause and Mr Job said *Praise be   She is back*

Mrs Tabitha come out of the kitchen with a smile on her face and a chicken in her hand. The chicken were not happy to see Cloe only because Tab had yanked its head off.

Then Mrs Tab seen my condition and the smile guttered some.

I will cook water for a bath

At the window of our attic I saw the top of Big's head just down to his haggard eyes – aimed at Cloe – half hungry, half afraid.

I climbed up to the attic for clean britches and found the rest of Big, robed in blankets like a monk – hair hooded – knobbed knees sticking out. I were no Baltimore belle in my soiled shawl but I did not wish to trade conditions with him. I were relieved to see him awaken from sleep all the same.

Big's face were hidden in shadow but I heard a grin in his voice at seeing my state.

You are used up, Meed

We make a pair

From inside the shroud came a mob of questions.

Who were that dandy making manners at the gate?   Where did Cloe come back from?   Did she not find the money I left her?   You have got a powerful smell   Where did you find her?   Why are you dressed so?   Is that s___ you are dipped in?   Is my name cussed around town for my failed bridge?

Every incident wanted a bit of explaining, and as I put down answers Big paced the attic.

The dandy were named Tom Tod.

I could not say where Cloe had been but Tom Tod were from somewhere else. He were on the canal packet with Cloe.

I knew this because I met them at the river landing.

I were dressed this way because Cloe did not care to walk home with a naked person.

I were naked because I had fallen into a puddle of s___.

I had fell into a puddle of s___ because I were after the night pigs.

The mention of the night pigs froze Big.

Too early for talk of the pigs, Meed

I know, but you will be glad to hear it for once—

I went along with my story slow, and cut out the part about how I had wanted a feat of my own on account of envy. As for why I had come to be in the graveyard at night, I said that somehow I got lost and turned up at Monroe-street. Big did not question it. The rest I kept true, and made into a comedy of itching and angry owls and tumbling from trees, then a regular sermon about how I seen how *night pigs are only regular pigs that we do not see right   On account of the darkness*   I paused a moment for drama. You have got to

156

mix different sentiments and styles in a tale, like cooking. *We are only afraid of being afraid*

At the end of my story, Big peeled the blanket back from his head – eyes wide as windows. *Meed   you got rid of the night pigs?*

   No, the night pigs are still there   It is only that they are not devils   Just regular pigs at night   One of them licked my face sweet as a pup—

I were swallowed up by a joyful bear hug – Big were not worried about getting s___ on the blankets. A hand come out of the bedclothes and shook me by the hair tenderly.

In the middle of this tenderness I felt a *snikpf* of guilt. Big had told me he feared busting up the pigs might bust up his spirit, and I had done it anyway. I had not meant the gesture that way at all – I did not mean to bust up Big – only to have a feat of my own. I did not know just what I meant to do.

After the tumult of returns and greetings and washing-ups Mr Job said we had better get after work, and chased the flock to their chores. Job Jr and Johnny was old enough to help with coffins. Mrs Tab gone back to plucking. Jonah, Joe, and Josiah squired Cloe as she gone to unpack. Little Jom and Joy wandered in the yard under the eye of their uncle Asa.

After my bath, I gathered up the makings of my almanac from the attic and headed for Dog's. All over Ohio and Cleveland folks gone to their work of a morning – preachers hunted souls and Philo made shoes and Ozias run his wagons and Dog made whiskey. All the world set to work, except Big, still in his blankets, watching out the attic window.

I were not a eighth mile gone when I heard Big hollering to wait. Still wrapped in blankets, on account of all his clothes being tattered, he were waving his own sheaf of papers. The shinplasters he had got for building his useless bridge – taken from Cloe's bed. I did not know that she had ever seen them. If Big felt sorry to have his gift spurned, his face did not tell.

A broad paw grabbed up the back of my shirt.

Come with me to Handerson and Panderson's, little brother

At Big's direction, grasshopper Handerson dove into the jungle and brung out a handsome set of the latest ready-made clothes. Big tossed some of his money on the counter and flung his blankets into the depths of the emporium. A leap into his new suit – he did cut a style in the looking glass. The shine even crept back into his hair some.

Handerson examined Big's banknotes and took on a sheeped look. *YOUR MONEY IS NO GOOD, BIG*

Big took this to mean the merchants was making him a present. *Mr Handerson I am terrible obliged   These britches will always hold a kind thought for you*

NO NO, WE ARE NOT MAKING YOU A GIFT   I MEAN YOUR MONEY IS SPOILED   IT IS NOT GOOD

Big stared at the greensuited merchant without malice

or understanding. *My money is spoiled,* he repeated like it were a school lesson.

EVERY LAST ONE OF THESE BANKS HAVE GONE BUST, Handerson explained. *THEIR NOTES ARE NOT WORTH THE PRINTER'S INK   YOU WILL HAVE TO GET OUT OF THOSE CLOTHES IF YOU WOULD*

Big did not quarrel. His pride had bumped its ass considerably, and promptly stepped out of the pants. *Brother help me find my blankets again*

Panderson hollered from somewhere in the deeps of the emporium. *LET HIM HAVE THE CLOTHES, HANDERSON   I HAVE GOT A PROPOSITION*

The advertisement were modest as such matters gone. TAKE IT FROM BIG SON   IF HANDERSON HASN'T GOT IT, PANDERSON DOES!! spelled in cheerful red on the backside of Big's new shirt. All the SONs was writ out in larger letters. As we walked to Dog's, Big judged he would never see his own back anyhow, and so had the better of the swap. The fact that his money were worthless did not seem to bother him much, although he said some cross words about Mayor Frawley.

In the thin light of the grocery Big looked at my rumpled papers with pride and fear mixed together. This were the first he had seen of my labors.

You are making an almanac   out of me? He whispered it like secrets.

Yes   I have collected stories out of folks I had not much considered whether Big minded being in a book, although the idea did suit his vanity.

What all have you got in there?

I greased my answer some. *Your feats and comic adventures mostly* I did not mention the various demises.

Big watched the papers intently – like they was racing roaches or a hand of cards.

What happens in the end?

Our family time ended when Mr Tom Tod busted through the door of the grocery in the company of none other than Mayor Frawley. The newcomer were changed into a suit the color of cider and stunk of toilet water to sting your eyes. His hands were busy slicing at a peach with a pearl-handled penknife.

For his part Mayor Frawley was holding his greasy hat and jawing that *this foolishness you hear about bridges will pass Ohio city is destined to be the greater of the two cities—*

Frawley! My brother threw the name like a brick.

The mayor put on a show for Mr Tom Tod. He sniffed some like he did not quite remember the name of this large, angry citizen what greeted him.

Yes Hulloa Ah Big yes good to see you returned Now Mr Tod as I were saying what this place needs more than bridges is investm—

Frawley

Beg patience Big I am conversing with Mr Tod

The money you paid me for that bridge is useless

The money were sound when I paid it to you   it is only as useless as your bridge

A good squabble were wasted without an audience – this one were witnessed by Dog sat on his stool – a sleeping Barse Fraley – myself – the cats of the grocery – the many ancient weapons hung from the wall – and by Tom Tod, whose whole face seemed to light up at the prospect of soured tempers.

You knowed that money were hollow Frawley   said Big.

I knew nothing

Dog screeched from his perch that this were *the first honest thing you ever said Frawley*

As Big and the mayor gone back and forth over whose wrong were worse, Tom sat down next to me on the bench.

Mr Meed, said Tom, his smile like soft wax. *Who is your compatriot?*

It is my brother Big

Tom chucked his peach, though it had plenty of good flesh left. *So this is the famous Big Son*

That evening, after Mr Job's scripture time, Cloe elbowed me and gestured at the smoking of a pipe. A quarter hour later we met up behind the barn. I were eager to know where she had been and what she had seen on her ramble, but she had another topic in mind.

You are collecting stories of your brother   she said. It were not a question.

A *snikpf* and the lucifer made a reflection in her eyes. Seemed to stick there some even as its fire passed into the tobacco.

I have got one for you   she said.

There is no Big Son at all   *There is only a sort of actor's costume*   *A shining wig and a neckerchief*   *And all those feats are just different folks*   *Regular folks, not spirits, dressing up in the suit*

    But how would the strength of a spirit find them?

    Folks forget themselves when they put on the costume   *Spiritedness hides in everybody but can only come out when you pretend*

    But   *who is wearing the costume right now?*

The fire of her pipe glowed orange and *fristl*ed.

It is only a story, Meed

There is no finer time than autumn. The very air is a refreshment – a washing out of your heart. But you cannot stay washed and autumn will not stay in place. Before long the bathwater grows cold.

Before long autumn will send you looking for warmer dress.

Ancient Dog kept the stoves of the grocery roaring at all seasons, on account of his hide being threadbare after seventy years of cussedness. The very air inside smelled burnt, but burnt were not warm enough for Dog. He were sewing up a winter coat such as Handerson or Panderson could never offer.

It was not a lie that Dog served in the rebellion against King George. Only he had not exactly fought but were a chore boy in an army camp. I do not know how he came to own a Continental Army coat, as he had never worn it in any battle. He only hung the mangy red-and-blue thing on the wall, pegged out like a pelt, and brought it down for parades and holidays.

I did not know what holiday he were expecting in early October but he took down his patriot skin and went after it with a sewing needle. I were back at the grocery working at the almanac, and Big with me, on account of he had no better use. I would scribble and try some of the stories on the ears of cats and loafers. Big – still gray hearted – would cheer some to hear his own feats. Dog sat at his mending and we made a regular family circle.

When I took a rest from my work, Big always liked that I read the news papers out loud. He had an idea that the papers would carry notice of troubles that might want Big's prodigy. I did not say that by the time a crisis has washed up in the *ARGUS* or *ADVERTISER* or *EAGLE* there is nothing left but a mess to tidy, but I done the looking-out all the same. A Friday noon brought the latest of the *ARGUS* – ink still wet on the page – I set aside the almanac to read—

MOBS GENERAL. A season of disorder across the nation. At Cincinnati an unlawful assembly attacked the abolition society in that place. In Boston a convent is attacked. In St Louis the land office and a news paper office. In Troy banks and courtrooms.

We are not so wild here, considered Dog, the exploder of bridges.

BOY WANTED. Luke Oakly is seeking an apprentice at cabinet making.

Big scorned the idea of a life spent making cabinets. I felt a small offense – coffins is only cabinets for bones. *Does no one want spirit work?* Big asked.

Professor Thompson will visit to talk on TEMPERANCE at the Sessions House hotel.

Dog shook his head some as if he were disappointed at this professor.

Kreosote.
FOR CURING THE TOOTH ACHE.
This substance of a recent
German discovery comes highly
recommended. It destroys the
sensibility of the nerve without
causing any pain.
Rely on Dr STRICKLAND for all
matters relating to the health,
preservation and beauty of the
TEETH.

*Will you be back to Dr S for
more kreosote?* I asked Dog.
   He looked up from
his sewing and grinned –
his teeth calicoed green
and brown with spots of
white left over from his
treatment.

ACCIDENTS.—YL Honey, a citizen
of Ohio city employed at the iron
foundry, had one hand blown off
and the other sadly mutilated by
carelessness in that place yesterday.

General sorrow at YL's
misfortune. He come in
for more than his share of
trouble in this life.

ON THE BRIDGE TROUBLE.—
Self-protection is a great law of
nature, implanted in the human
heart for wise purposes, and is
a principle which will, and must
be, called into exercise, not only
in defence of life and limb, but
also in upholding, what is in many
instances, equally important, our
dearest rights and privileges.
It gives us pain to have any thing
occur, calculated to excite ill-blood
between these young and thriving
cities. Their interests are nearly
identical. Their prosperity—

Gasbagging over the bridge
were the chief occupation
and diversion of news
papers on both sides of the
river, always using ten cents
of talk where a penny would
suffice.

BOULDER TROUBLE—From
Hinckley. The improved road to
Medina is stricken. A collection of
large and obstinate rocks tumbled
from Whipps Ledges and efforts
of draft animals and man are
ineffectual in remov—

My brother grabbed the
news paper and slapped his
eyes to the bulletin.

I could hear Big's mind chewing the news from Hinckley. His hair glinted some touch in the slanted grocery light. I seen a mood rolling into his mind – from familiarity I known how certain of his tempers troubled the air just before busting loose.

Dog hopped down from his stool, his bones clacking together.

Finished with the f____r

Every eye turned to see the wormy soldier coat, held up with mean pride. It looked just the same as before, though we complimented Dog's work anyway.

Same as Big pulled the newspaper from my hand on Friday, he yanked me from sleep on Saturday. The sun were still abed and only a few birds discussed the day ahead. The bird talk were joined by my brother, who clucked *Up up up* even as he drug me down down down out of the attic to the yard.

In the scrambled mind of waking, I thought to find Mrs Tab and her corncakes – drink a ladle of water – do some stretching and scratching. But Mrs Tab and the cakes were still abed too. Before I could do anything at all, Big shoved a mattock into my hands and hopped on Agnes. He grabbed the back of my shirt and sat me behind him. I wondered if Agnes shared my same fogged brains.

A galloped mile clears the head, and after the sun begun its climb, Big explained his haste.

The news paper said there is Boulder Trouble out Hinckley way

He did not say any more. I could mark his thinking plain as Handerson's writing on the back of his shirt – a road choked with rocks were appetizing work. It were a happiness to see my brother puffed up, and I were glad to ride as deputy, though I were not certain what I were wanted for besides witnessing.

A dozen miles up and down gentle slopes, through thick

woods speckled with farms and stump-stubbled clearances. As we *thuk*ked along I were sure that the very leaves of the trees was blushing from green to gold to crimson as we passed. Agnes came up a rise and I saw around Big's shoulder and out over the treetops. The land went forever. You felt awful small in such a wide country.

A dozen more miles to the tidy, tiny village of Hinckley, then a mile more to a churned-up place where great shale rocks broke through the soil and made a devil's playground. Our ride ended at a narrow pass, where stones the size of wagons had busted loose and bowled into the road.

Big leapt from Agnes without slowing and dashed toward the boulders like they would run off on him – leaving me to catch at the bridle. Agnes were lathered and somewhat cross at the extent of the ride. As I gone to tie her up she chomped at me and I cussed her. But our quarrel were forgotten when the *thuk*s of another arrival boomed.

We scampered up the stones to meet a man thick as a chimney, climbing off a gray draft-horse. This new man had no neck – no narrowing at all between skull and shoulder, only ropes of muscle lashing brains to body. His galvanized hair were silver and his shovel-shaped beard were silver and his clothes were mossy – like they had grown on him. His great gray horse surely had an elephant in its family tree. The pair of them made ferocious stares at Big.

Hidy stranger   hollered Big.

The man nodded sternly.

Would you be the Stoat? my brother asked with a hungry grin.

A second nod, sterner than the first.

In Ohio city, we had heard a tale or two of the Stoat from farmers of Richland county. The Stoat's feats was honest work – useful and sober. Plowing a dozen fields in a day – kicking stumps clear over the horizon – catching up every crow in the county and lecturing them on leaving corn alone. I had worried we might encounter Feathers – the wicked spirit of Hinckley. The Stoat were polite company in comparison.

Hollering up to us from the road the Stoat suggested they work together, but Big insisted on a contest. The Stoat were reluctant, but with no stakes made and no gamblers around, he allowed there was good fun in seeing who could crush boulders faster.

Even after Big said *Go ahead* the Stoat did not move with much haste. He climbed down to his side of the pile slow, and went to fetch his pick-axe slow, and walked up to the rocks slow, like he meant to preach at them. He swung back his pick-axe slow too. That were the end of slow – the tool came down with a ripping snort and *kshrik* sang off the rock walls around us. Big watched the Stoat go for a few swings before he joined, with his mattock saying *fshink* back.

It were a strange hymn – the only words *kshrik-fshink* and

again. I do not know what the two meant to praise. I clambered up the slope and found a perch to watch Big go.

As the sun climbed even farther, the sound of Stoat's pick steadily chewed boulders to gravel. Big kept pace but his breathing were heavy.

kshrik-fshink

Even at noon the day were cool but Big were leaking rivers of sweat.

kshrik-fshink

The Stoat's great gray horse and Agnes mowed the grass on their sides of the boulders – waiting for their masters to finish fooling.

kshrik-fshink five thousand times.

Before long I turned my attention to the clouds passing over the blocked road – great white flesh shaped like bread. I considered I were hungry and wished I could eat grass like Agnes and the gray.

kshrik-fshink
kshrik-fshink
kshrik

The Stoat kept at his swings even as my brother went to poor behavior. Big sat down in the dust of the road – gathered up his knees and put his head between. He stayed there long enough for a cloud to pass halfway across the sky. When Big finally stood up, he stared at the boulders for a time, then leapt atop them, with his chin poked out, hair shining, lip quivering.

Stoat   We might finish the work sooner as a team after all

I could not see the Stoat from my perch, but the *kshrik*s did not slow at all.

Stoat   Let us tear down a tree as a clobbering stick and pitch the stones to each other   We will make a new game of who can clobber best

There were no answer but *kshrik   kshrik   kshrik*

I do not know if Big's pride broke on the work itself, or on being outworked. But it made a sorry mess either way. One of the great bready clouds crossed the sun and a chill leapt into the air like it had been waiting for the chance.

Stoat

kshrik

F___ you Stoat

I could not see the Stoat but the *kshrik*s finally ceased.

You heard what I said   Big snarled.   You are invited to offend yourself

I could not hear the Stoat, but his response were clear enough from the result.

Big leapt at him from the boulders, diving into a fight like it were water.

By the time I scrambled to where I could spectate, the Stoat had grabbed Big by the legs and swung his head into the boulders. Big hopped up – shook the ill use from his brains – grabbed a rock the size of a raccoon. Whatever had darkened his heart had restored his muscle some. He fired that rock and a dozen more at the Stoat like cannonballs. The rival spirit dodged and danced splendidly but one soon

171

caught him at the joining of his legs. For a man with no neck the Stoat could sure holler. He let out a sound I cannot properly describe – like a cow at the bottom of a well.

That were only the first of it. They kicked and hollered and knocked each other to sawdust for an hour or more. A steady tornado of teeth and hair and stitches of clothes spun up around them. They pounded each other to such extents that each flew apart and flew back together with some of the other's parts mixed in. So wild was their brawl that they fixed the trouble without meaning to. The two spirits smashed each other into the stones over and over that the boulders were soon minced to gravel. Their stupid conduct gone on a while more.

Once the road was passable the gray wandered over to Agnes and chewed grass near by – the two stood head to head like they was in conversation. I wondered if the great gray horse asked Agnes what made her master so ornery, and whether Agnes might not share Big's poor mood. She did not act out any though.

Only after a quarter hour did the Stoat mark that the work was done. He raised a hand to halt. Then Big seen it too. Heavy swallows of air from both, and awkward laughter from Big – the church organ wanted tuning. His new clothes were ripped to bits. All I could read of the advertisement were SON HASN'T GOT IT.

With Big asleep behind me on Agnes, I had ample time to wonder on the long ride home.

I wondered whether the Stoat were hard up for feats in the same way as Big. I wondered how he were paid for his work.

I wondered why Big had brought me along. I were no use in clearing rocks. Perhaps he brung me to trap the tale and put it in the almanac. I did not think I would, as Big's conduct had been so poor.

I wondered what had curdled Big's heart. I would have liked to ask but he were fast asleep, snores tickling my ears, breath brandied with shame. Perhaps the day's disgrace did belong in the almanac – showing how pride were worse than whiskey – how a man who wants glory too much will only fetch shame. There were a comic aspect to the incident, too.

At the barn I found Asa hosting a visitor – a tall and proud stallion the color of cider, wearing a fancy five-dollar saddle embroidered with PRESIDENT ANDREW JACKSON in silver thread. The whole horse looked like he were fresh bought from a store – Asa eyed the glowing guest with polite caution, and Agnes greeted them both with haughty snorting.

I slid out from in front of Big and let him slump forward onto Agnes's broad neck. It were a relief to get from under his sodden bones. I tied her up and set out a late supper. In her eagerness to dine she pranced some, enough for Big to shift a bit – and a bit more – and he molasses-ed right off Agnes and landed with a gentle *fumpf* in the straw and s___ of the barn floor. Big did not mind the fall any.

It would take a second set of hands to get him up to the attic.

In the family room I found the seven young Stileses gathered around a vast game of marbles – a rare and wicked delight to have marbles run to such a late hour. There were an eighth child as well – Mr Tom Tod in a suit the color of port wine. Tom were right in with the little ones, on his knees shooting. I also seen that the game were conducted with brilliant agates – the finest marbles I ever saw. I felt a poke of jealousy.

Tom were the first one to greet me, like this were his home and not mine. There were rubies in his pitted cheeks, and he held up a jug like it were something he had hunted.

Medium, join us   Have a sip of health

The marbles and Tom were not the only new notions. Around the room I saw a pair of silken handkerchiefs on Mrs Tab's lap. She looked terrible sore at the heathen practices under way, but she were holding her tongue for some reason, and only angrily sewing. Mr Job were asleep in his chair with the Bible spread on his lap like a blanket – I spotted a fine new folding knife on his knee.

Cloe were sat as far as she could get from Tom without taking to the ceiling or leaving altogether. I marked a fine brush with a pearl handle clutched in her hand like a hammer. Behind the chatter of marbles and the stink of Tom Tod's cologne water, the air were strangled some.

Strangling aside, I considered it rude to dismiss Tom's offer to sip. As I tilted my head back I could see Cloe and Tab staring knives at my manners. A scale or two fell from my eyes and I realized I had walked into a sitting-up. Tom had come to court Cloe, and Cloe had asked Mrs Tab and Mr Job to linger, to avoid the courting. I did my best to disappear into the game of marbles – better to act a child.

The shooting had come down to Tom – who did not consider marbles at all child's play – versus Jonah Stiles, the champion shooter of young Ohio. Before long, I forgot the sore manners of the courting for the drama of the match. Even as Cloe stared at the fire and Mrs Tab stared at her needle, six children, one Meed and one Tom watched Jonah's steady thumb strike the winner.

Aw s___, laughed Tom. *Let us play again and put some skin on it*

He dug in his pockets for money, but the cussing had finally torn matters for Mrs Tab.

MR TOD thank you for your visit So much pleasure leaves us tired out and we must have our rest I do not know that we deserve your many presents but we do thank you

Tom remembered himself some and put his money back into his pants. *Enjoy the gifts is all the thanks I want ma'am The hour surely is late* he said.

Tom expected he were being left alone to court Cloe, and only caught on slowly that he were spurned.

I had better see Andy Jackson home

Without stepping one hair closer than she had to, Cloe shoved the gift brush into his hands saying she *could not imagine keeping such a rich gift with no way of returning the gesture*

I haven't got any gift half as pretty as your smile Miss Inches   All the reward I want, Tom said back. He did have a style to him.

Cloe looked more likely to go for Tom with a hatchet than give a smile.

I chased Tom out into the barnyard hoping he might help drag Big up to the attic. Mr Job were asleep and Mrs Tab were on her last worst nerve and I known better than to mention Big to Cloe in her present mood.

Mr Tom   can I ask a private favor?

Under the moon his whole aspect changed. The rubies were gone from his porridge skin and his suit were changed from wine to the color of rabbit guts. I imagined his pride were pinched at the edges some.

Mr Tom   would you help me put my brother to bed?

Tom did not answer right away. As he eyed up Big, still abed in the barn mess, a smile like a rat's tail curled across his chops.

He looks content where he is

With that Tom put his boot to Big's head and used him as a block for climbing on golden graceful Andy Jackson. He swung the stallion around like they was dancing and went from the yard as smooth as a marble rolls.

*

176

August Dogstadter had a way of walking you could spot a league off. Every stride were a different length, and he looked unsteady, but like a drunk dancer, he had the utmost confidence. His footfall were faint, like he only just touched the ground. Quiet or no, you could not miss him.

The sentries at the bridge marked Dog approaching long before he hailed them. They swapped fearful looks over the tops of their muskets. Dog's contempt for the bridge were common knowledge on both sides of the river – as were rumors that he was the fiend behind the bombings.

To have him walk up at midnight – dressed in his red-and-blue patriot coat – waving a jug – were a considerably ill omen.

Good evening f__kers   in a hush croak.

What do you want here, Dogstadter?

I mean to use the bridge to cross the river   *I am too old to swim*

The sentries looked at each other.

Trail arms, cretins   *I am only going visiting*

The last time you come visiting the bridge were exploded

Not me, lads   *Only visiting friends*   A wave of the jug in his hand. *Go into my pockets and see if you find any barrels*

Up close Dog's frailty were hard to miss – the glaze in his eyes and the spots on his skin. His tongue were dangerous but his old bones were nothing to fear.

The guards stepped aside and the voice come out from the booth.   *Five cents*

* * *

The bridge men were not scholars. They did not think how it were awful late for social calls or that Dog did not have any friends anyhow. The hour were odd, but ours is a free country for good and bad. The old bat had as much right as anyone to use the bridge as long as he did not try to explode it. Besides, look at him wobbling like he had busted spokes – dressed up in his old soldier's uniform – living in yesterday.

What is there to fear from such a used-up sort? Besides, it were poor manners to refuse a patriot.

As Dog paid the toll to the invisible man in the cabinet, a salamander look run across his lips. He ambled out to the wooden draw at the center and gave the moon a gracious bow. He set down his jug and proceeded to strip out of his clothes – like he meant to dive into the river for bathing.

Dogstadter has finally lost his mind, said one of the sentries.

It run off long ago   He is only missing it now   said the voice inside the tollbooth.

I wish he had left that jug behind   said the other sentry. *Let us have some peanuts*

Peanuts are a penny

In the moonlight Dog's threadbare skin had the color of dead wood – his shed clothing at his feet like fallen leaves. Standing over his shed skin, Dog brung out a knife from I am not sure where and set to slashing at his prized soldier coat.

He poked and punched and ripped his coat into rib-

178

bons, all the while hopping on this foot, then that. With cheerful hums that carried across the water, he strewn the pieces into a posy-ring. After a bit of this maniac dance, he reached for his jug. He did not refresh himself but instead he poured a toast all over the remains of his army frock, skipping around the circle like spring's very maiden.

With the jug empty, Dog crouched down and then came a *snikpf* clear as church bells. Sudden as a roach he run to the edge of the bridge. It were a startlement to see how fast he climbed the railing and over – just a glimpse of his bare shriveled ass catching the moon as he dove. Before you even heard his splash, the red and blue of the soldier coat turned to wild orange and the flames coughed *krtHNGFNG* – before you known it the whole heart of the bridge were burning.

The night has only got one eye to watch with. On this particular evening, the quarter moon had a great deal to consider.

All in the same night, it saw Tom Tod step on my brother's beanpot.

Saw the naked Dog make a fiery furnace from a suit of clothes.

Saw the bridge burn yet again.

I apologize to the moon but there is more veils to lift.

You will pardon bragging but making Dog's soldier suit into a bomb were clever. A dozen pockets and pouches added to the inside and filled with gunmeal – and a jug filled not with whiskey but with Dr Strickland's kreosote – which burns wild and fast.

You have got a question. How is it that I have such good tales of Dog's explodings?

The night of July 3 – carrying barrels of powder down the hillside in a parade of fools.

In the September rain – Dog riding a wagon-bomb.

And now – his October bonfire.

I ought to have told this a while before.

I were with Dog at every exploding.

You are cross with me – I know it. Rightfully. But hear my confessions.

The first exploding were only a demonstration, and half of the west side come along – Barse – Philo – Ozias – YL – even Absalom the mule and fat old Oliver. It were not half as evil as you think.

The exploding in September I gone because Dog asked, and I were always liable to folks asking me – and because Mr Job setting me to make the almanac poked a bruise on my heart. I were proud of Big, but that storm of envy were well along – the one that would soon carry me to Monroe-street and my great trial. My manners and good sense was busted some by volatile emotions. Surely you have felt such a way.

Before I explain why I went along with the third exploding, let us haint through time for just one moment. You recall my night among the tombs. How I seen that night pigs is only day pigs dressed up in our fears. How I lost my britches.

I got my britches back but I did not collect myself entirely. Ever since that night I could not stop my mind from running after a dozen different ideas like four-legged dogs after squirrels.

Big and I would leave Ohio for the west and find him more feats.

I would leave Ohio alone and find my own feats.

Big and Cloe would leave Ohio and I would make a life without them.

Big would leave, and Cloe and I would make a life.

Cloe and I would leave.

The third exploding I gone because I liked to.

After Tom Tod used Big's head for a stool, I did not have time to get Big up into the attic. I did my best to bed him down in the straw and hurried to meet Dog at the grocery.

Now, I am not a maniac for NONE. Two bridges or twelve. Rivers are meant to be crossed. I do not pretend that exploding the bridge ever made sense. Not even Dog would lie on you so bad. He would only say he liked to blow up what vexed him. Violence sometimes works like leeches – spill some bad blood, to speed the good along. But the contempt over the bridge were past reason.

I believe that Cloe came near some invisible truth when she imagined that Big Son is only a costume. A suit that folks put on for courage. Only Cloe did not go far enough in her claims. I think we all are forever looking for costumes. We are naked and fearful fools in search of disguises, with pockets to hide our sins in. Actor's rags. I were swapping between coffin maker and brother and biographer and apprentice felon freely all summer and fall – and there were more actor's clothes besides.

The coat-bomb awoke the night to screaming – screams of *FIRE* and *TREASON* and *BUCKETS* streaked along the east side of the Cuyahoga. Four-legged dogs took up the cries and then church bells joined with their own barking. At night you cannot see smoke but you can smell its merry stink – the great orange eye of the burning bridge admired itself in the dark river. It were a handsome vista, enough to distract folks from my climbing down to the riverside. There I played the part of Pharaoh's sister and grabbed up Dog from the reeds.

Sleep fled before I had enough of its company. It were not singing birds or the light of the sun that woke me but Mr Job's shoe – knocking on my ribs.

    Meed   Get up

Mr Job stood over me, curled forward some, eyeing me like I were a mess to tidy.

    I need you as a carpenter today

    Mr Job   it is Sunday   and besides I ought to finish up the almanac

That looks to be more than enough   He eyed up the pile of pages next to my straw. *I think you have hunted everything worth eating out of Big   We will take it over to the* ARGUS *offices tomorrow*

Downstairs, the whole homeplace were boiling with work. Cloe and the young Stileses made busy gathering saws and mallets and boards – even littlest Joy carried a load. Mrs Tab were stuffing folks with corncakes. Asa were already hitched up to the cart and watching the corncakes carefully. The chickens seemed serious in their peckings, and even Big's snores of *brrrghhg* from the straw had an industry to them.

I yielded to Mrs Tab when she came after me with the cakes. As I chewed I asked what had bit the household so.

Snakebrained Mr Dogstadter has exploded the bridge again   she said. *And on a Sunday*

No   When will this madness end?   I acted the part of innocent keenly, in my estimation.

Madness is the very word for it   Besides cusses, said Cloe as she swept past under an armful of lumber.

I am going to bury this peabrained feud with hammer and nail   said Mr Job as he shoved my apron into my hands.   *We are going to mend the bridge as an apology to Cleveland and then we will have peace*

I realized what mood were on Mr Job – he had reached the place beyond the shroud of silent judgment. Where he were become agitated enough to tell you his mind. This place were visited only rarely but from my youth I did recollect that it often was accompanied by a sore bottom.

Before five minutes gone, Mr Job had chased me, Job Jr, John, and Jonah onto the wagon and gave Asa a *huphup*. We clattered out of the yard even as Big tumbled down from the attic, still pulling his britches on.

All of Ohio were stirring. The trees and their dying leaves were restless in the wind and a gang of four-legged dogs rumpused through the lane – dashing under and between Asa and the wheels of the cart and causing Mr Job to yell *Whoa now*

Just then neighbor Dennes hollered from his door that *goddamned Dog done it again*

We have got to put law on that creature   Mr Job hollered back.

As we swung into the lane I looked back and saw Big back in the yard, chewing a corncake, surrounded by chickens. He had a particular dip to his head, one that meant that he were experiencing a notion.

You can imagine what the idea were—

Big had woken up on the barn floor, with his brains fogged by the Stoat's fists and his face decorated with mess. He had climbed up to the attic for more sleep, but before long Mr Job were rousting us, saying the almanac were finished, Big were hunted out et c.

The only thought on Big's brambled mind were to find just one more feat. That were his concern as he straggled down to the yard, where he saw the household abscond in different directions – kitchen door whanging shut, Asa's cart clattering out – and the only explanation he got were Mr Dennes *goddamn*ing a pack of rumpusing dogs and Mr Job shouting back that *we have got to put law on that creature.*

Big looked over at Agnes, who tilted her head just the same way.

When the Baptists first put their church up in Cleveland they took to theatrical gestures to grab an audience. I do not judge them for it. Only I will forever recall the first baptism they did. They had opened for business at January of 1833, and the preacher declared that he would make his first baptisms in Lake Erie – nature's vastest bathtub.

Lake Erie tends to have a dress of ice at that time of year, but the preacher went right ahead. On the appointed Sunday he wrapped himself up warm. If a stranger come asking for his cloaks and coats, it would have taken 'til Monday to finish the robbery. He led his flock out a furlong onto the lake's frozen face. They swung picks to make a holy font – the cold coming off the water must have bit at their very eyes.

A crowd of curious eyes from both sides of the river gathered around the hole to see how Baptists done – and the preacher begun his show. Fat as a fall squirrel in his coats he gone down on his knees – grabbed ahold of the first sinner by the underarms – lowered them into the lake's greenblack eye. I swear the water made a sound like *snikpf* as they gone under.

A tidy pause and up come the redeemed – their white

gowns soaked through – their eyes bulged out – their teeth going like popcorn. The crowd made eyes right back, watching carefully for the holiness.

ANOTHER HOLE.

Near to five years later some of the same folks stood on both sides of the hole in Mr Clark's bridge, wearing the same Sunday faces. Two dozen feet down, past the scorched and splintered timbers, the snot-colored river peered back at them, just as curious. Dog's coat-bomb had blown away nearly all of the bridge's draw – just enough of one railing survived for someone to gingerly make their way across – but no farm wagons would cross to Cleveland today.

Asa tugged the cart up to the edge of the crowd – just as curious as folks to see the elephant. He snorted and shook his ears as *begyourpardon* but there were no room. The crowd were thicker than bugs on butter. Mayor Frawley – Philo – Ozias – YL Honey, his blasted hand still bandaged – Mr Clark's orphans, draped in damask – Dr Strickland and Barse and Tom Tod – and across the hole were half of Cleveland.

Confronted with what they cannot fathom, folks turn to what they know best. So Philo and Ozias went to squabbling.

This is the work of the devil said Ozias.

You flatter the deceiver *This is the work of white men* frogged Philo.

Ozias considered this briefly. *The devil IS white*

Philo somehow took offense at this. *The devil is all different colors* *Speckled like a snake*

188

This set Oze to screeching.   *O you are a scholar of devils now?   No the devil is white   He were once an angel and angels is white folks   He might could be French—*

The devil cannot be French   He speaks English   He has got to speak the same language as God

I tend to agree with Ozias that the devil is a white man. Not because the devil is clever or the devil were once an angel – though both are true enough. Our devil is a white man because the devil looks like what you seen in a mirror-glass. Besides, I had it on confidence from my brother – who met the devil, you will remember. Big said the devil were just plain folks.

Philo and Ozias were only amateurs at jackassed talk compared to the two mayors.

You are always free to soil your own britches   but now you have soiled mine Frawley, bellowed graybeard Willey from the Cleveland side.

Willey you know this is not my work   This is fool's madness
Just last week you vowed to tear the bridge down by November

Frawley made to protest but had no ground.   *That was   only bluff*

Your bluff is called by your own August Dogstadter   You lose the hand

Frawley scratched at an ear, like Willey had bit it.   *You are not wrong but   that does not make you right*

Tom Tod – in a suit of daffodil yellow – suddenly went to Frawley's side and counseled him. The lanky Tom bent

189

down and whispered into the badger's hurt ear. I could not
say if the dandy advised Frawley or made him a Punchinello.

Tom to Frawley, inaudible:	Frawley to Tom, sotto voce:	Frawley to Willey, shouted:
fsst fsst fsst	*I don't want to say that* *Fine*	*You are—*
fsst	*No goddamn it I will* *not say it*	
A look of reproach	*Goddamn it*	*You are right* *This is idiocy* *Both sides have been* *idiots*
fssssssstfsst	*No I won't say it*	*Ohio city have acted* *and continue to act* *as idiots more so than* *Cleveland* *You may consider this* *an admission that Ohio* *is at fault*
fsst fsst fsst fsst	Nodding	*We will never make* *money in these towns if* *we are always cleaning* *up such messes*
fsst	A look like he meant to puke his breakfast	
A last barrage of *fsst* and several sharp gestures with a forefinger – at the bridge – at the river below – at his own crotch and then finally at Frawley's forehead	*A thoughtful* *grimace*	*Let us have* *negotiations toward a* *marriage of the towns*

A tumult followed – a regular charivari pan-banging. Hollering and large gestures. Stomping of feet and arms thrusting skyward. It were a surpassing rumpus. What Tom and Frawley proposed were for Ohio city to own that she were the little sister, once and forever.

Dog did not mean for this   I said – not minding that it were out loud.

He has mistaken himself awfully   said Mr Job from next to me. With that he grabbed a saw and mallet from Asa's cart and set to chasing folks off so he could work.

I went to the wagon as well but stopped to watch a brown dog race toward the crowd. The animal streaked past the back of the gaggle and went right along the flimsy railing that remained on a side of the scorched draw – nearly knocking YL Honey into the hole. Poor one-handed YL hardly noticed the dog blazing past, as his ears was being separately chewed by Philo and Ozias. He never seen the second dog coming at all.

Chasing its comrade, the yellow dog barreled into YL's legs and sent him into the hole in the bridge. Hardly anyone marked the sound of his splashing into the river. What was observed was the sound of a hundred more dogs, heading down the hill, their barks a lunatic choir. At their head were Big, hollering and swinging his arms and laughing as the voice inside the tollbooth cried that each creature owed five cents to cross.

*

The story took some patching together from those who seen different bits, but the Club for the Detection of Horse Thieves was not wanted to solve any mystery. My brother must have heard Mr Job declare *you have hunted everything worth eating out of Big* from where he slept below. He had woke up desperate to have just one more feat.

With his head still clouded from the Stoat's pummeling, Big had mistaken two-legged *Dog* as four-legged *dogs* in Mr Job and Mr Dennes's hollering about putting law on creatures. Big were often a fool, but not an idiot. He put his brains to the situation and considered that a four-legged dog will not know to follow a regular written-down law or sheriff's sign. But you could get a dog's attention with smells every time. So he had just got to talk in smells. I do not mind saying that his plan for the dogs and my plan for the pigs shown a certain shared sophistication.

Big went into the kitchen and found himself a piece of salt pork and rubbed it all over like Tom Tod's perfume water. He got that pork inside and outside his tattered shirt and on his hair. Once the scent was good and fixed, he went on a triple-time march around Ohio city, visiting every roosting place familiar to dogs – mostly meaning rubbish piles. The plan were a ripping success from the first. Before he had gone a half mile, a dozen dogs. A half an hour and he had enough dogs for a revival meeting. Beggar dogs – pet dogs – cur dogs – dogs of every size and manner – Democrat dogs and Whig dogs – yellow, brown and black dogs.

Remember that the coin has two sides – my brother were

not an idiot but he were certainly a fool. He had not thunk out what to do once he had all the dogs. But there are situations where you cannot admit of doubt, or the whole enterprise will falter. So he did not stop to seek counsel. In fact he only took on more confidence. He met a few folks around town who did not care to see the exploded bridge, and they laughed at his dog flock, and a few brought out jugs to toast. You cannot deny a sip when you are toasted.

That colored his mood as he and the dogs stormed the bridge. Forgetting poor YL in the water below, folks made way for them, and the dogs streaked across along the narrow sliver of bridge. Big himself broke into a run and leapt across the gap – making a cannonball of himself – and bowled into a thicket of spectating east siders, who clucked at his wild manners.

The procession did not halt to beg pardon – they galloped across the river bottoms and up the bluffs – circulating through the Sunday streets of Cleveland – followed by folks glad for something to do besides counting up sins – myself included.

Ours was a good-natured invasion. We gone to the Public Square and marched all around it a dozen times, making more noise than Dolores the cannon and collecting more critters and a few children. If Big were worried at all on how to fix law on the dogs, he did not let on. Marching and merriment on a fine fall day was purpose enough, until matters turned sour.

That moment come when Big brought his flock past the Baptist church at Michigan- and Seneca-streets. It so happened on the Sunday in question that one of the foremost Baptists in Cleveland – Mr Basil Clam – were marrying off his daughter Ebizaleth to the wheelwright Fert Derby. In fact, Ebizaleth were already round some in the belly with the latest of Fert's wheels. But folks was not rude and only said that pretty Ebby were still growing into her womanhood. On account of the cheerful church music and murmuring crowd, my brother could not resist paying his respects to the wedding.

So my drunken pork-smelling brother and his brigade – and myself – barged into the church at the precise moment of the preacher cinching Ebby and Fert as man and wife. The whole assembly went quiet with the work of believing their eyes.

Big were very happy to see so many friends from the Cleveland side, and all dressed up so nice. But he did wonder why all their finery was topped by curdled faces. Why had Ebby keeled over? Why did Mr Clam issue such a fancy curse? Fert were more forgiving and acted that he were flattered to see my brother. *Hidy Big   Good of you to come*   even as Ebby were going to the floor with a rustle. After Fert spoke, the silence come back, broken only by several of the dogs lapping at the holy water.

This were not the first nuptial gathering my brother wrecked by mistake.

There was the time he had fallen through the roof of the Episcopal house during a wedding – but only while retrieving a kite for some children. In fairness to Big, that roof were not carpentered well and he had been after a good deed.

And the time he chased down a spooked horse and finally brought it to calm in front of St John's. Now, this were no crime, except he had been at his washing when the horse run off and was wearing only shirtsleeves, and his hind and front bits were visible all around just as the wedding party come out. Men frowned at Big for a month after that, and some women still did not return his hidys.

And the time Big gone on a spree with Squirrelcoat – a spirit whose every garment were made of . . . squirrels, little pelts all knit together. For all the practice, Squirrelcoat's skills as a tanner were poor. He did not get all the blood and guts off his pelts or let them cure enough. As a result he smelled slapping bad – folks said his stink could curdle milk in the udder.

Squirrelcoat were strictly a rascal spirit – only after mischief and merriment. He and Big Son had met by happenstance and liked to see who could roll a stone farthest – a game of bowls! Soon enough a stone were rolled into a tree what crashed in on an outdoors marrying picknick. Big and Squirrel behaved honorably and helped pull folks out from under the branches, all the victims in their best, spotted with blood and picknick foods, their eyes wide at Squirrelcoat's stink.

In truth, Big had a compass needle under his hair what steered him toward weddings. He hardly ever busted up a funeral or a sing or a dance. He did not mean bad by it, I do not think. It is too easy to say his faulty needle come from the crisis with Cloe. Were he acting as a child, busting what he could not have for himself? Was it pulling braids and shoving into mudholes all over?

Whatever drove Big, the incident with Fert and Ebby went past suffering for some folks. Mr Clam were not the wealthiest man in Cleveland, but he were close enough to toss an axe. He agitated loudly against my brother, saying *Big Son ought to be in chains* et c. Mr Clam were not alone in sharp talk. I heard folks ask for the first time whether Big might be happier elsewhere. Such sentiments thickened in the following days. Folks asking about Big – considering his prospects – lamenting his sidewaysness – regretting him.

Big were not present to mark all the broil – he were seen to ride off that Sunday, jug in hand, with the look of a spree on him. It is good that he cleared out for a time. Otherwise he would have itched from the ears awfully.

Even with Mr Job, myself, Job Jr, John and Jonah all taking up the work, it took several days to mend the busted jaw of Mr Clark's bridge. I found the work a satisfaction – I had not forgotten how to carpenter wood while I were lost in the almanac. To bend my arms and gulp down the fall air, which tasted of brass somehow. The sound of sawteeth comes to feel a second breathing, the very babble of your blood. *Workworkworkwork*, is what sawteeth said.

Oh f___ is what Jonah Stiles said. His saw had busted apart, and the blade tumbled down into the water with a slap.

Mr Job slapped with his tongue.   *Jonah Stiles I will take back the teeth and tongue I begot in you if you do not cease cussing*

I am sorry father   It is only that my saw—

Never cuss your tools

Yes father

Not five minutes later Job Jr stepped on Jonah's hand and another cuss flew.

Jonah!

You said never to cuss tools   Job Jr is not tools

If you can't speak politely, then cease entirely   Do not say a word   Where did you find that putrid language?   Was it a gift of Tom Tod?

Jonah did not know which of his father's orders to obey. *It weren't Tom*— he begun before realizing the only answer worth making were *I am sorry father*

As we sawed, mayors Frawley and Willey haggled how the two cities would unite – practical matters such as wards and councils, and what to do with a second mayor when you have only got one city. Squat surly Frawley said they ought to be brother-mayors, like the old Roman emperors. Willey politely invited Frawley to return that idea to his rear end. Frawley then asked whether they might split up the mayor's mantle – Willey taking four days a week including the sabbath, and Frawley the remainder.

Such practical questions only held the mayors' attention briefly. The real questions were matters of pomp and pride. What would the new city be called? Old man Willey thought *Cleveland* suited just fine. Frawley asked if they might stitch the two names together into *Ohioland* – or perhaps a high-toned coinage like *Frawlepolis* – anything but just *Cleveland,* which suggested Ohio city being swallowed up. Willey did not care for any of these points.

With the bridge ruptured and commerce slowed, both sides of the river turned to the business of talk. The staple crop of all seasons – talk of fast horses and pretty girls – talk of whether Dog had died or only disappeared – talk of newcomer Tom Tod and how he had such deep pockets – talk of how *Tom means to make Cloe Inches his bride   You mean Cloe Stiles   No no she is an Inches   I seen what inches of her caught*

Tom's eye   that catfish   The sound of men laughing like meat frying. Hushed talk of a manner that were never dared around Mr Job or Big – but I have always had nimble ears.

Men did not bother hushing talk of Big. He were off on his spree still, and there were no point keeping confidences, so general were the sentiments – that he were not worth the lamp oil to look at – that to have *a spirit who don't do feats were like a mule who don't haul   You cannot teach a mule indoors work   You cannot teach his meat to eat good   But he still wants his hay*

You can only cut such a creature loose

Folks east and west put no trust in Dog's actual demise. They agreed that living or dead he was now an outlaw, witnessed at his sin. Mayor Frawley even allowed sheriffs from Cleveland to search the grocery for the missing Dog. But he were never seen after his dive into the river. The grocery was peopled only by cats and a few faithful idlers – whiskey widows who helped themselves to merchandise, promising to pay Dog if he ever lazarussed.

Confess it. You have thought at least once in your life that matters might go easier if a certain person died. You do not wish them dead. You would not say it aloud. You would not murder them. Only thought that if fate did strike them down it might grease matters favorably.

Confess. I know you well enough by now.

Such were the case with Dog.

Both sides of the river seemed relieved at his vanishing. It were poor manners to swing an aged patriot at the end of a knot – no way of respecting elders, even spoiled ones. Putting Dog to trial would have only soured the wound between towns.

*   *   *

A feeble peace prevailed once the bridge were mended again. The public view in Ohio city regarding the union of cities softened some, from an *outrage* to an *unpleasantness* to perhaps a *tolerable wrong*. Dog's absence helped keep the peace, although Cleveland could not forget the sour grapes entirely. The bridge guards kept teeth on edge – belts full of knives and guns – eyelids nailed open. Every wagon that come near the bridge were searched. Every man and woman wishing to cross made to take off their shoes and empty out their parcels. It were a wonder that the guards did not skin folks to look for a bomb in their guts.

The sin already done is the one we look for sharpest.

After God rousted Adam and Eve, He put an angel at the gates of Eden to keep them gone. I imagine that angel stood around – sweating some on account of the flaming sword – stuck in his own tollbooth cabinet – his face never seen. I wonder how that angel passed his days. Whether he ever wondered why the Lord had him mind an empty garden.

October encourages a bird to abscond from Ohio in favor of warmer air. By that month's end, most every winged thing obliges, excepting for chickens and finches and the idiot geese that emigrate from Canada in great caravans. One gang of them chose the Stiles homeplace for their winter quarters. Every morning these surly invaders strutted around the yard, waiting to seize the breakfast corn from the chickens. Cloe would hiss at them and chase them off, and the dance would resume the next day.

There were one especially bold gander among the visitors. At first he only *skronk*ed at Cloe like he were demanding satisfaction. Then he took to chasing her. He did not go after the corn or bother the chickens any – he were fixed on Cloe and could only be discouraged with a broom. With each successive day the gander grew bolder – stomping on his blueback legs right at her. Cloe would laugh at him, and even his *skronk* had something comic to it. The entire homeplace came to appreciate his awful manners. We even invited Mrs Tab to watch his bravado. She did not smile but I swear I seen one corner of her mouth twitch.

One day the goose did not charge Cloe at all, but simply walked in a wide circle around her into the kitchen. Cloe, myself, the chickens, and even the other geese watched him disappear into the doorway.

A moment after Mrs Tab made her own *skronk*.

Cloe   the bird
Yes mother
What does he want?
I could not say
Fetch me the hatchet

At the very moment Mrs Tab thunked the roasted gander down on the table – minus the impertinent brain – the grinning face of Mr Tom Tod appeared at the back door.

Ah   a picture of surpassing domestic bliss   His hat lifted
two feet over his greased hair. *My greetings to you all*

Mr Tod, were all Mr Job said by reply. He and Mrs Tab dis-
approved of Tom for a number of reasons by now.

Tom were wearing his heaviest manners. You could near
to smell his scheming.

*Forgive me mother   I see you are about to dine   I did not
think of the hour   I will return tomorrow   It is only a matter of
town business to discuss with Mr Stiles   What an ambrosial scent
is your cooking   My own dinner will seem poorer for having had
the pleasure of sniffing   Evening to you*

Mr Job twisted his mouth a bit. He did not like to be rude
– Tom had counted on that.

Would you join us Mr Tod?

The gander gave one final impertinence – his flesh ate like
wet rope. This did not keep Tom from eating up two plates-
ful to flatter Mrs Tab. Even as he fought to swallow the bites,
he spread oily compliments around the room and fixed his
eyes at Cloe. Big were still off on a spree, which were just as
well. Had he seen how Tom stared, a broil were likely.

After a polite agony, Mr Job moved to see Tom off.

Mr Tod we will sit by the fire and you will tell me your business

The men gone off to jaw, and Mrs Tab and the children
chased up chores, and Cloe grabbed me.

Meed   give us a smoke

*   *   *

Walking through the barnyard, I saw Tom's Andy Jackson tied up between Asa and Agnes. I could tell Asa were bit with jealousy.

Behind the barn Cloe and I blew up a great cloud of smoke, colored blue by the stuffed-full moon. I hoped the moon's dinner were better than ours.

I cannot abide Mr Tod   Cloe announced from her side of the cloud.

His manners are awfully rich   I allowed.

His eyes are always stuck to me   He makes me want to wash   From the very first I seen him at the canal   I liked to be shut of him

Puffs of smoke.

Cloe   You never said where you run off to last time   and how you came to return on the packet

Deliberative puffing.

I never went anywhere

A quiet came over to my end of the cloud. How do you tell a person their memory is busted?

You were gone from here for all of August and a spell more
I were not
I seen you come off the packet with Tom   I were naked and you gave me your shawl   How could I misremember that?

I were not on the packet   I were only at the landing   and Tom Tod only grabbed on to my skirts like I stepped into a mud-hole   I were here the whole time

I did not understand what Cloe meant. She had been

gone – I knew it from reading her letter by mistake – from Big's woes and her empty bed.

I got my mouth opened up to talk but my tongue did not find hold of an idea. Cloe let me dangle for a moment before explaining how she *were only hiding   I stole one of Mrs Tab's great bonnets as a disguise   And gone to Cleveland   And took up as a helpmeet there*

My mouth were stuck open again. Cloe known what I meant to ask, which were *Why?*

I only wanted to be myself
But you were someone else
Only my Cloe   and not your Cloe

Just as the sound *your Cloe* touched my ears, shoes clomped across the yard, headed for us. Cloe rushed to drop her pipe and arranged her skirts over it. For all her courage, she feared to be caught smoking.

Mr Job come around the corner – first his hunched head, then the rest of his matchstick self. *Thought I might find you two here*

Yes father   We are strolling to aid digestion while Medium has his pipe

Come inside once you are digested

Even with the moon at Mr Job's back I could see a half smile as he turned to go.

And Cloe?

Yes father?

Your skirts are on fire
Oh f___

Mr Job paused. It were the same cuss little Jonah preferred.

Back inside there were several dispatches from Mr Job's talk with Tom Tod. <u>One</u> – the two mayors had settled on the first of January as the wedding day for Cleveland and Ohio. <u>Two</u> – Tom Tod would put on a great husking bee and frolic on the first of December to celebrate the impending union. <u>Third</u> – Tom Tod had asked Mr Job if he might have Cloe's hand in marriage.

Cloe – still smelling of burnt skirts – had a sharp laugh at the last bulletin. *Rather give him a foot to his marital bits*

Manners Cloe   scolded Mrs Tab with half her heart.

I counseled Mr Tod he courted you at his own risk   said Mr Job. *You can put your hands and feet where you like* *but* *Putting Mr Tod aside* *it is time I said it* *you ought to marry someone*

You ought to marry Big   Mrs Tab poked into the talk.

I ought to make my own choice   Cloe poked right back.

A familiar lyceum took up – mother and father reminding Cloe that she would have to take a husband one day – that she could not stay at home forever – that Big had a good heart and a broad back – that she might save Big from himself.

Cloe reminded them that she loved Big as a brother only. For my part I said nothing. Only felt a sickness wash about my guts. I were not sure if it were the notion of Cloe marrying Big – or Cloe marrying anyone – or the unruly gooseflesh from dinner.

After an hour of Mr Job's reading from the book of Isaiah, my insides still felt sour and I took myself to bed – where I found Big returned from his days-long spree. He were sat at the attic window, whittling by moonlight, smelling of drink, wearing half a beard.

Hulloa brother

Hidy

I do not know if it were my stomach or the full moon or just my natural sin but at that very moment I tasted a bitterness in my blood. In that moment I hated my brother for the first time. The hate did not hold – it only had puppy's teeth. But I had felt it and could not forget it.

What were the scripture tonight?   Big asked as he scraped at wood.

The puppy teeth again. *Mr Tom Tod has proposed to Cloe*

Big's whittling stopped.

I did not tell him that Cloe had snorted at the idea of wedding Tom. I did not tell Big that Mr Job and Mrs Tab wanted Cloe to marry him. I only crawled under my blankets and left him to fret.

Before dawn put a rosy finger on Ohio I were bit again –
not the puppy's teeth but a shoe into my ribs and a foul-
smelling whisper of

S___head   wake up

I peeled an eye and saw only shadow. But I knew who
were inside the dark. Dog hung over me like bad luck – his
breath were better than cold water for waking a body.

*Dog   you should not be here   The homeplace will wake soon
and Mr Job will find you*

*Old Dog is slicker than owl s___   Job Stiles will never know
I were here*

You are supposed to be drowned   you must go

*I got restless being drowned   and I heard that the cities are to
wed in January*

Drowned folks have keen ears   You must leave

We will bust up the wedding   You will help me

No

*Should I ask Job Stiles to volunteer you instead?   Tell him
that you proved so useful at the other bombings?*

My brain were hollowed out. Only the sound of Big's
snoring. *Brrrghhg*

*Do you hear me Mr Medium Son?   Or should I ask Job Stiles?
Ask me what?*

In the faint light I saw Mr Job stood at the top of the ladder – one arm full of papers.

Love and tenderness come along slow like a good stew. But you can make a meal of unhappiness quick as you bite from an apple.

Mr Job were confused by the voices in the dark – at what sounded like a conversation.

Who are you talking to Meed?

I did not know exactly who I was talking to.

I helped Dog blow up the bridge   I am snakes in the manger

A bite of apple for everyone.

Dog vanished to smoke before Mr Job could reply – which were some time coming. The shroud of silence come on terribly. I imagined I could even *see* the shroud over him, fluttering some in the attic draft.

From inside that burying sheet something flown down toward me.

BIG SON'S ALMANAC 1838. – new ink still damp.

I thought you would like to see it   Mr Job said.

Let me explain

You will read it elsewhere

Mr Job let me—

You will read it elsewhere and sleep elsewhere and work elsewhere

Father—

Get out of my barn

Vol. 1.]   "GO AHEAD!!"   [No. 1.

BIG SON'S ALMANAC
1838.

OHIO CITY

LAKE   ERIE

Containing Adventures Exploits Sprees
& Broils in Ohio, &
Life and Manners in the Northwest.

Ohio city, Ohio. Published by Job Stiles. See Page 2.

Before Hiram Spurgeon run off, he worked as a farrier, minding the feet of horses. He spent all day tacking on traveling shoes but never went anywhere. Perhaps the *tacalatacalatacala* of all those journeys haunted his brains.

Perhaps there is no haunting to it at all, and Hiram only wanted a son. By keeping horses in shoes Hiram kept a wife and a tidy home and a growing flock. Seven daughters, each pretty as a May daisy. Three boys, all taken back by the Lord before a year.

On the day his eleventh child were born – another girl – Hiram Spurgeon suffered some type of rupture. No one can say if he ever learned the sex of the last child. Only that when his eldest daughter come to fetch him home, the fires in his shop were still warm – his tools laid out – his shirt and britches folded up on his anvil. Hiram himself were entirely gone, having only taken his own shoes with him.

You would have to find naked Hiram Spurgeon to ask him the true meaning. But generally I hold his tale to signify how family is at once too much and not enough. In honor of Hiram, we made a Webster's word of his name. To SPURGEON were to quit your kin.

You can be an orphan from more than parents. You can be an orphan from friends – from coffin-making – from Mrs Tab's corncakes – from the company of Asa – from the rustle of Cloe's skirts as she gone about hard work – from seven little Stileses – from an untidy brother.

In truth I never felt an orphan from my blood mother and father. I were too young to know what I lost. I remembered them only as clouds. There were no such cloud hiding the Stileses. My exile hurt much worse than puppy's teeth. It felt more like putting my face on a grinding wheel.

I made Dog's empty grocery my Babylon. There was whiskey enough to sell for months, so I opened the doors and took custom in Dog's stead. His demise had not spoiled the thirst of the grocery idlers, and I were glad to have Barse and YL and the other whiskeyheads and the cats for company. I even had a touch of pride at seeing how many read the almanac I had made.

Dog were never seen when custom were present. But at night he come out and murmured at me with a stove's heat. He always and only talked of his final exploding – the grand ghastly gesture – at times I wondered if he had been a night-

mare devil all along and I had never marked it. In truth I
felt half a haint myself.

Hainting to the side, I proved out as a whiskey grocer. The
idlers and loafers brought in a steady income. The cats
accustomed to me as their boss. Before November were out
I felt landlord enough to change the sign over the porch
to M SON GROCER. I hoped that Big or Cloe would call,
so I might show them how I done – and so I might hear
of the homeplace. I knew from talk that Big were gone to
shambles, and I knew from manners that a woman would
never set foot in a place like Dog's unless they was hunting
a wayward husband. So I did not expect brother or sister to
darken the grocery door. I settled for keeping up with them
by rumors.

I heard Philo and Ozias before I seen them – three leather
shoes and one wooden leg on the porch.

I do not say I care for Tom Tod   Ozias screeched as they
come in the door. *Only that I back him*

Backing is the same as caring

*You have got all five of your toes in your ears, Fish   I mean I
would bet Tom over Big   That does not mean I like him   only
he is more likely*

*You would bet that narrow dandy versus the man who rastled
an entire lake?*

A woman's heart is not a lake   Fish.

I should put you in a lake   Basket.

Mr Phi's manners suggested he were overdue for refreshment.

Hidy Meed   A jug

People cannot help themselves but bust in two. God himself grew bored of Adam and made an Eve for entertainment. People will rupture over anything at all just to have a contest – which horse is fastest – Vanburen versus Harrison. The great hot-air debate that November were Big versus Tom for the prize stakes of Cloe's hand. It did not matter that most folks hardly knew Cloe past a hidy and a hat lifted. It did not matter that she despised the very idea of marrying. Facts will not stop folks from wagering and busting-up. An opinion prevailed that Cloe would relent – submit to marriage – from weariness if nothing else.

Neighbor Dennes came into the grocery and reported that *Mr Tod is practically an eighth Stiles   Job cannot keep him away   I swear I seen the dandy leap from bushes to court Cloe*

Ozias took Tom's persistence for prowess. *You see the dandy has iron underneath   He cannot be stayed   And where is Big Son?   Pissheaded in a ditch*

Black-eyed Eli Frewly were accorded a measure of special insight regarding Big on account of having been pummeled by him more than any other man. Eli held that *Big keeps an awful envy under that halo of hair   There have been other suitors   And he has discouraged them*

I recalled then how Eli had once brung Cloe a basket of vegetables and awoke on the roof of a church the next day, with an empty basket and a sore skull. Big had been careful that Cloe never heard.

Alvo Farley observed *Tom Tod has got the mayor's ears in his pockets*

Philo asked *What has a mayor's ears got to do with lovers, you lump?   Cloe despises Tom   She will wed Big   She is only stubborn*

Alvo were winding up to cuss Phi when Birt the soiled preacher put in with talk too vile to write down. His sentiments hung like burnt hair before Mr Dennes spoke again.

I half expect Mr Tod waits in the privy house for Cloe   Every time he comes he has got gifts for the entire house   Bonnets   Knives   Dolls   Licorices   He even brung a bit of maple candy for old Asa

My heart ached at that last one. Tom were too fresh – miles past.

Cheerful Dr Strickland told that *Tom has had the kreosote at least three times since September   I do not mind the custom but I do not know if such vanity is entirely healthy*

Mention of the infernal kreosote reminded me of Dog. I swore I heard him stir in his hiding place below.

The idlers turned to a general consideration of how Tom come by his circumstances – how he kept his pockets so full.

Round merchant Panderson said with pleasure WE CAN-NOT KEEP THE YOUNG MAN AWAY   YOU ARE ALL INVITED TO SEE THE MERCHANDISE THAT MR TOM TOD PREFERS   He lifted the jug and without delay crickety Handerson took up *Teneriffe wines patent medicine febrifuges butter cranberries brooms of first quality paper hangings—*

Handerson cricketed this way for some time. I wandered into my imagination – saw the homeplace sieged by Tom – Mrs Tab boiling mad, stabbing at her sewing – Mr Job reading his Bible harder and harder as if it would chase out the trouble – Cloe refusing to acknowledge Tom at all – the children greedy for gifts – Asa at the kitchen door for more maple candy.

I asked whether Tom Tod were courting Cloe or courting the esteem of others, if Cloe was only a looking glass for courting his own self. His vanity went past pride and come close to a worship. There were not a believer in Ohio city's five churches with a stronger faith in God than Tom Tod's faith in Tom Tod. But at least he had faith.

Handerson were still murmuring his inventory when Mr Dennes said *I do fear she might kill the suitor sooner than answer him*   From his way of talking I suspected Dennes would not hurry to find the sheriff in such event.

You might ask her yourself   said Phi with his eyes pointed to the door. *She is hitching up Asa at the porch*

My mind forgot the ruptures and rumors the moment I heard—

Meed   half hollered.   *Would you care to step outside of your   location?*

216

I near to fell from my stool in haste. Cloe and Asa and all seven little Stileses!

Cloe:	The children:	Meed:	Asa:
Brother!	*Meeeeeeed —* seven times over	*Cloe — Job Jr —* *John — Jonah* *— Joe — Josiah —* *Jom — Joy*	A snort
A pat of the arm and a kind look	Jom slid from Asa's back into mud, to his delight	Head pats and chin chucks	A shimmy

Cloe!

It is good to see you   You are missed

It is a balm to see you all and the old oaf   I went for vigorous scratches behind Asa's ear.

My   how you stink of tobacco and   men

Begpardon   I do not know if she ever marked any odors of mine before and I felt a pride at catching her attention so.

I am sore at you besides your stink Meed

I had wondered what Mr Job had told her.

Father will not say why you left   Only that you sinned awful   And lied on it   And were not fit to share a barn with livestock lest they take sick with your poor character

He does not lie   I am sorry over it

I did lie. At that moment, I did not feel sorry over my banishment. Besides, there were creatures in that barn with far worse character than mine — chickens do not have any character at all, for instance. But I had sinned. I would go that far with Mr Job.

Cloe only patted one hand to her guts and the other atop it – like some business had been swallowed and would not be talked of again. She leaned forward to say *Now let us have a smoke*

You would come inside?

I would not   You know better than to ask

We will smoke here in front of the children?

We will not

To the alleyway then?

Yes

What about the children?

Asa can mind them

The alley beside the grocery were no Shangri-la but I did not mind. As I smoked up a cloud I realized I did not know what to say to Cloe. I thunk of the blockheads inside. They would be in knots to know what odds Cloe herself made on Big versus Tom.

I hear Tom Tod has made a pest of himself

Cloe puffed.   *I should like to murder that man   I do think it is the only way to make him stop talking*

Have you declined him?

I have declined his proposal a hundred ways but he does not listen

Cloe chewed the insides of her cheeks, and I let talk of Tom blow away.

*   *   *

Asa did a fine job of minding the Stileses' flock. He may
not have realized he were minding them, but he had done
it all the same. The little ones were climbing all over and
under him, chasing each other, flinging mud. Uncle Asa
only shook his head in disapproval of horseflies.

Or perhaps he were in disapproval of the company. I saw
that Tom's Andy Jackson were hitched up down the rail. I
knew a rotten love-apple were soon to fly through the air.

Cloe were restoring the littler ones to Asa's back when
the love-apple landed at her feet.

Miss Inches   let me help you

It were Tom Tod, of course, dressed up in a suit the color
of plums.

Mr Tod   I should not like your help   You could feel the
lye in her voice.

I would be a heel not to offer it

You are already a heel

Tom raised his chin in mock affront. Cloe did not look at
him – only gone back to sorting out the children with a fury.
I found I were grabbing hold of a porch post.

*Miss Inches   To see you with the children   you are the very
picture of motherhood   It is a sin to deprive the nation of—*

Mr Tod I do not require your company any

Let me win your heart

It is not a thing to be won

Let me steal it

It is not a thing to be stolen

219

Let me—

My heart is pledged elsewhere   To Big Son   Iwishyou-goodday

I swear Tom Tod's pox scars scrambled around some on his face. The tidy notches of crystal fell to disorder. My own heart did some circus riding as Tom bowed and went back inside.

Cloe grabbed me by my shirt. *You will not tell your brother what I have said*

As Asa led the cart full of Stileses away, I thunk on what Cloe meant. You cannot keep a marriage a secret – certainly not from the person you mean to marry.

Cloe's words had plucked Tom's pride, at least for a moment. Back in the grocery he sheeped some as folks settled up bets on the courting. But a moment later he went right into gasconading like it were ointment.

Boys I have been spurned by maids in Newyork Pennsylvania and Ohio and sure as the Lord made women fools I might be spurned in every state to Arkansas   He were back to himself. *But this bachelor will always stand a jug for every fool here—* A chorus of drowsy cheers. *Let us drink to the marriage of towns!*

Not a moment after I closed the grocery up for the night, Dog swung open his cellar door, wrapped in a mile of blankets against the cold. The cats ran to greet their ancient friend with mayows. He did not speak a word but soaked up the stove-singed air. Only when he were good and warm did he spill out the cusses he had barned up.

F____g Tom Tod talking on union in my f____g grocery

Every November night Dog rose and gave such whippoorwill songs.

In the beginning of TWO BRIDGES OR NONE, I figured Dog only wanted there to be no bridges at all. But his late outlook suggested NONE gone a great deal farther than bridges. Perhaps there should be no Cleveland at all. I wondered how long before he banished counties and states – banished Columbia – banished the whole world – only kept his stoves and felines.

I did not know whether he would banish Meed as well. But our evenings were serene enough. I nailed up the shutters for privacy, and we made family sitting hours each night, lonelier than the homeplace but livelier too. We would drag coffins over to a stove and read from a greasy book of Shakespeare – comment on the human condition – sip refreshment. We passed most of November this way.

* * *

As a grocer, you learn the different ways folks hold their whiskey.

Some folks swell up until they are tight for space and take to fussing. Some go silent. Some feel a particular hunger for food or company. Some folks only tiny their eyes and go stupid.

Philo fashioned a bridle from whiskey. That were how he kept life from bucking him.

Barse leapt into a drunk with gusto – it were always *so far   so good* with him.

Mr Job, I remembered, frayed at the ends like a cut rope after too much drink. He did not cuss or tell scabby stories, but he would smile at talk that his sober self reviled.

Whiskey would stretch my brother like a long shadow at dusk or dawn. All his gestures and sentiments grown to twenty feet tall from their usual ten.

When I took drink, my brains burned like a wick.

Dog never showed his whiskey too obvious, but his hide did soften a ways. For a wild murderer he were more companionable than you might credit, not at all deaf to other hearts. In our evening sittings he liked to poke at my melted brains and give interpretations thereof. He were as keen as a preacher at understanding folks.

So I poured my worries out for him.

That I were banished from the homeplace and my heart were sore over it.

You would not have helped me sin if you were happy

That Big were pinched between man and spirit and I did not know where he would find happiness.

You do not know if you can be happy yoked to him

He even saw in me sentiments I never said out loud.

You are three times in love   And three times spurned

I have courted no one

You love your brother too much for wanting to be him   You love Cloe too much for wanting to have her   And you love your-self most of all   Because your brains is the one place you cannot swarthout from

This had the reek of truth, though I did not like to say so.

You do not believe that   You do not believe anything Dog

I believe in plenty   I believe in myself and I believe in Ohio city

But now you want to explode Ohio city

A place has got no meaning apart from what folks do in it   And I would have my doings remembered like a bruise   Like how you made that almanac as a coffin for your brother

He is not dead

He is dead enough   We are come to a day of dollars and steam factories and not spirit piss

And what day do you belong to Dog?

They might get me dead but they will never get me buried

I were about to lawyer with Dog that he were already buried – when a thumping came at the door.

I were careful with the shutters and Dog always kept his voice quiet. I did not worry that this midnight caller would know I spoke to a dead man. I hollered that *we are closed to custom* but the thumping persisted and took a voice—

Medium

It were Mr Job. I could swear I heard refreshment in his voice, the sound of which put sentiments on me. I would see Mr Job. I would stuff Dog back into his tomb and—I turned to see that Dog had already vanished.

Hidy Mr Job

I realized he were not refreshed at all but ill – his nose red and running – his body wrapped up in several coats and scarves besides.

Hulloa Meed   I felt glad at the switch from *Medium* back to *Meed.*

You are not well

Only a fever

You will come inside and warm up

Mr Job set down a knotted kerchief on the table next to one of the boss cats. The burly orange tom squinted at the bundle, suspicious.

I made to fetch a jug but Mr Job made a gesture for me to sit.

Meed   I cannot find your brother   I have not seen him since three weeks   Has he been about?

I shook my head with a child's obedience.

I suspect he will turn up here sooner than the homeplace   He is heart sore over Cloe and knows I have a scolding for him

I went over to nodding.

You will give this to him if he turns up   He picked up the kerchief and dropped it down with a *klunfk.*   *I know how curious you get   so I will spare you peeking   It is three hundred dollars silver*

I swear that tomcat's eyes went wide. I know mine did.

How did—

The almanac

I stared at the money harder, like it might grow a mouth and affirm Mr Job's story.

There is a comedy to it   Folks have never liked to pay your brother for his feats   And you know how scarce hard money is   But folks on both sides of the river   Folks passing west   Folks from the farms   took after those almanacs like sugar   The man from the ARGUS could hardly work his press fast enough

With that Mr Job stood up. *Mother Tab will be wanting me back home and resting*

You are leaving this here?   He had explained it already but—

I should not trust you after your dishonesty   but I choose to anyway

He left a last thought with the silver.

Meed   when I knocked   you answered <u>we</u>   Who is your partner?

Dog rose from the cellar wearing a mile of crooked grins.

Most folks leave their money a jug at a time

I suppose it is not Mr Job's money to keep

What will we do with it?
It is not yours any Dog
Is it yours then?

The rest of that family hour was quiet. Dog gone about tidying before climbing into his moldy bedclothes – he reposed hardly two feet from a stove. I would have feared another person's burning up, but I do not know that flames could hurt Dog.

My stove that night were cold silver, and I sat awful close too.

I am not an expert at drinking. I do not do it regular enough. I am a poor hand and I cannot find any peace in it. Drowned Dog cannot die by fire and burning worries cannot die by drowning. I dunked them in whiskey all the same.

Three hundred dollars is only thirty pieces with some centuries of banker's interest. Am I clumsy to mention Judas Iscariot? This bit of money is not more from the devil than any other dollar. I do not expect any Gethsemane tonight. I only want to use Judas and his story for thinking on.

Judas goes in to the high priests of the temple and says *What will you swap for Christ?* and they offer thirty pieces. Poor Judas does not haggle any – he does not hold out for more – even though he has got them by the toes. They do not seem to know how to get Christ any other way. No other disciples are keen to bargain. Poor business by Judas, done by heart instead of brain.

Mark says that Judas hanged himself in shame, and his silver bought a public cemetery. But Acts tells that Judas bought up a prime lot and gone to farming, only his guts exploded and made him into manure. It is a confusion.

I do not expect that Judas escaped damnation. Only I think that the scripture has barbered the story for fitting into pockets. I wonder on Judas and his hopes. What did he want to do with his silver? What did Judas live on? Did he have sons and daughters? Did a Mrs Judas comb out her hair and sing songs of an evening? Why did Judas go for sin except to teach us lessons? Who is he without us?

The money is at least half mine. There is no almanac without Big's feats, but neither is there any Big without my almanac.

Ohio is half mine.

The future is half mine.

Cloe is half mine.

If I am owed so many halves, I ought to take all the money and not consider myself piggish.

If you read your own wanting enough times, it will smear like news paper. You will not know what it ever meant.

On the insides I am as tall as my brother. My hair brighter, seen a mile off.

Desire is unlettered. Ask Asa why he cared for sugar.

You consider me worse than Dog and his exploding.

A person is only a bank paper. Only an idea and not hard money, subject to speculation and bust.

I do not mean to talk sour.

Home is all burned up. I will depart. I will make manners and go west. I would be very glad to see the angel on my way out. Shake his hand. I never thought on how an angel's hand is. Roughed from whatever work an angel done. Warm as guts from that flaming sword.

I will promise to write the angel. He could read the letters at family hour except he has no company.

I would walk west, naked as Adam. Naked except for the money. I will take the money.

Dawn has brought cannons and bombings and shoes into my ribs just in the short time of our acquaintance. I would prefer all of that at once to the whiskey sick of December first. Waking stood on my chest with both shoes and went after my brains with a sledge. I squeezed my eyes hard to banish the world. But you cannot shut your ears.

Mayow, said the grocery cats.

Little brother, said Big.

Hidy, said a voice I hardly knew as my own.

Big were soiled considerably. His last encounter with soap was some miles back – his hair a greasy crown. But circumstances were congenial, and he and Dog sat over a breakfast of coffee and cold pork. They did not speak to each other, but only eyed up the ten-dollar silvers stacked up like cakes.

Meed we are rich

Who were *his* we?

krTTHWANNFFNG	*bwong*	
	bwong	*bwong*
krTTHWANNFFNG	*bwong*	
	bwong	*bwong*
krTTHWANNFFNG	*bwong*	
	bwong	*bwong*

First banns is not yet a wedding, and a wedding is no July 4 or Washington's Birthday or Perry's Victory. So you should not have Dolores fired twenty-six times for the twenty-six sisters of the republic.

This was my sore brains talking.

Oh, go ahead and fire the cannon. These banns marked more than an everyday wedding. For two cities and seven thousand people brought together, go ahead and have Dolores and the church bells, and Tom Tod's husking bee. I did wonder if Dolores were saying YES or NO to the nuptial. A person might hear what they like in a *krTTHWANNFFNG*. Different hymns to the same music et c.

This were not a proper two-sided banns. Only the bride's family would gather at the husking bee. Bridegroom Cleveland would hear no dissent. It is all only theatre besides. Tom's were not even a true husking bee – he had not grown one ear of this corn and did not need our help. He had bought up ears the month before and kept it by. This were a pantomime of real husking. But folks should not deny any cause for merriment, especially at the doorstep of winter.

So tie red and white and blue ribbons onto every hat and bonnet and bridle. Scrub faces clean. Lay by chores. Come down to Ozias's barnyard, made up into a palace. Brush out the mules and wash their teeth. Light a hundred lanterns. Bring out fiddles. Put wax to your hair and climb into your finest shirt.

Mayor Frawley made sure to read the banns right away before folks was too refreshed and rowdy. He hauled his badger self atop a wagon and went to hollering.

CITY OF OHIO IT IS MY PRIDE AND PLEASURE TO ASK YOUR PERMISSION FOR THE MARRIAGE OF YOUR-SELF TO YOUR SISTER THE CITY OF CLEVELAND

Frawley did not mark that marrying your sister were considered poor manners.

ON THE FIRST DAY OF 1838 THE TWIN CITIES OF THE CUYAHOGA WILL BECOME ONE THE GREAT METROPOLIS OF THE NORTHWEST THE TRUE HEART OF THE REPUBLIC ONE GREATER CLEVELAND

A polite huzzah. No cusses of dissent. Dog were no longer with us to protest. All else who had backed NONE swallowed their contempt to spit another day at some other mortal affront.

Frawley gnawed the air for a while longer about limitless prospects and inevitable prosperity. But I did not mind him any once Big arrived to the festivity, hidying me with a slap on the back. He looked a far cry from this morning. His hair were brushed out and shining like brass, and his smile rode atop the reddest neckerchief I ever seen. He had taken some of his fortune to Handerson and Panderson for a proper set of readymade clothes, and the new getup rustled like straw as he moved. He were back in his power for the first time in a year. What a medicine is money.

But Big's coming into fortune had not repaired his reputation. Soreness lingered over the bustings-up – undone feats – nuisancing – theft of dogs. As we laughed at each other's dandyism and lifted a sugar-sling, I marked mean eyes cast Big's way. Myself I did not feel the puppy bite over silver or Cloe or anything else. My inside goblins were behaved for the occasion. I wanted to congratulate Big on his betrothal, but Cloe had swore me to secrets about it, and I kept honest. I were out of that habit, but I had not lost it entirely. Strange that Big himself did not mention his own banns.

I did not see Cloe or any of the little Stileses, or Mrs Tab, or Mr Job – sick at our last meeting. Perhaps the whole homeplace had taken ill. Or perhaps they did not want anything to do with Tom Tod's celebration.

Tom shone worse than Big's hair – like he had won five fortunes. He wore a boiling white suit, and I swear his pox scars had done themselves up into handsome patterns and curlicues. For a moment I felt a gift of omens and I saw the future of Tom Tod. He would fatten up into a Mr Clark – a great white hog, chewing brandied dollars all day, atop a hill, alone except for his servants and silver.

For now he were only atop the wagon with Mayor Frawley, who were finally running out of words—

And now I have said my few thoughts   I should like us to hear from our benefactor   who stood us to this celebration   To the sugar-slings and cakes and merriment   Before we set to husking   let us give Tom Tod our EARS

Groans gone up at Frawley's comedy, then cheers for white Tom.

Hidy to you all Ohio   Thank you to our eminent mayor for saying all the boring bits

Laughter and a badger frown.

I will not challenge him at prattling   I will only say the rules of the husking   The man who shucks the most in a half hour wins the stakes   A forty-dollar horse   and the honor of representing Ohio at the formal ceremony of union on the first day of 1838   at the center of Clark's bridge

Robust cheers.

One last bit   For each red ear a man finds, he wins a kiss from the maid of his choosing

Further hooting and a rush for the heap of corn. Big did not budge and I stayed with him. Normally a derby or contest of any type would fry Big's blood. But coming into expectations seemed to have banked his appetites. He looked peaceful almost.

* * *

You have never laughed until you saw a husking bee. Men yanking and twisting like they had a thousand fleas – dashing to gather more ears – fighting each other over corn. See Alvo Farley with a spooked-horse eye and Eli Frewly's bald head shining with sweat. YL Honey, his blasted arm still in bandages, ripping at ears with his handsome kreosoted teeth. Kerm Basket, older brother of Katie – and Richard Fish – Bill Gutkint – Lem Freeley – a dozen more. Tom Tod himself jumped into the bee, but he were only playing. He mostly watched and guffawed. When he did shuck an ear, it were somehow always a red one. He made a show of surprise before eyeing up maids like merchandise and finally taking his kiss.

Every husking bee I ever seen followed the same story. At first the gladiators keep to their own husking. But if you see a rival is badly outhusking you, clobber him to slow him some. And then when you and your rival see that a third man is pulling ahead, then you join to clobber that fellow. And then you are clobbered yourself. And so on until corn is forgotten in favor of a general rastle. This one gone the usual way – it was Eli going for Alvo that started it. Then the two of them grabbed up Richard Fish – and then Kerm – and Lem – and a fracas commenced. Before ten minutes had passed, only YL and Tom still husked. Tom was roostering around collecting his kisses mostly.

That were how singled-handed YL Honey outhusked twenty men. After the counting-up, Mayor Frawley went to raise up YL's hand like he were a champion rastler but only found the stump wrist – which he raised anyway.

In the midst of backslapping and recalling the choicest moments of the brawl – Kerm had bitten Alvo on the seat of his pants – Tom Tod come over to Big and myself. Red corn were falling out of his pockets and his pineapple cheeks glowed with kisses.

Friends, I am glad to see you here   Medium and Big   celebrated Sons of Ohio   soon to be Sons of Cleveland   let us anoint the occasion and celebrate your fortune Big   I hear the great Columbian eagle has made a nest in your purse

Big grinned, half sheep half wolf. I drew a ladle of sugar-sling and we passed it around.

We drank to Big.

I put up a toast to Tom, the emperor of kisses.

We drank to Tom.

I considered it were time to drink to Meed, but Tom said we ought to drink a second time to Big and his engagement to Miss Cloe Inches, that Tom *would trade all these red ears and a hundred more for the affections of Miss Inches   but you have conquered her heart   A drink   To your luck in love*

Big froze with the drinking spoon at his mouth – a good amount of sling poured down his chin. He did not stop to wipe before bolting the barn in the direction of home.

The first drips of dawn brought Big back to the grocery. Even in the thin light, I could see his pride were dimmed again – his eyes red and his head hung low. It were not hard to detect who had battered him so.

He spoke uncommonly quiet and slow.

When Tom told me   I rushed for the homeplace and ran the whole mile   I found Cloe at the stove boiling sap to make a specific for Mr Job's ague

Sugar mixed with clear corn liquor remedies most any illness.

And I dashed in the door to embrace her   And she smacked me across the eyes with the spoon

I could not help an inside smile.

I do not recommend sap for eyes   I hollered a fair amount   Cloe knelt to dab at my face with her apron   and made apologies   Only that I had startled her   I forgave her   even though my eyes did hurt awful bad

I had mistook Big's red eyes for heartache, not scalding.

I forgave her and said that Tom Tod had spilled her secret   And that I could not contain my joy   That I knew the Lord had sent three hundred dollars for reasons past my knowing

I did not ask how, if a thing were past knowing, he could know it.

She gone quiet a ways and stood up and turned her back to me   I thought she were weeping with too much happiness   and I went to finally get that embrace   and she caught me in the ribs   I fell over into the stove and spilled the sugar and scorched myself further   Cloe did not rush to help me   To pat out the sparks on my new clothes   I looked up and saw she had put on her school teaching face

She said <u>Big   Tom has played a cruelty on you   I will not marry you</u>

and I said but I have got true prospects now I have got three hundred dollars

And she said <u>I were not waiting for any prospects   I have answered you true from the first</u>

And I finally known she meant it   But I only had a moment to consider it before she hollered at Asa   Asa had let himself in the door and licked up all the sugar

My inside smile died at an instant. Too much sugar would put the bloat on an ox.

I were too sorry to much mind Asa   but Cloe would not listen to another word from me   Banished me to the barn attic   And I gone up to our roost and stared at my money   And asked it what to do with myself   Before any too long I heard an awful groaning from below   It were poor Asa   his belly all stretched out and aching

I went down into the barn and the whole household were at Asa's side   Even Mr Job wrapped in his sickclothes   They done what they could   Cloe cut into Asa's paunch and put in a quill   The gas come rushing out and made a sound just like a whistle   I

*went back to my bed hopeful that Asa were saved   Hearing his
cheerful tune   but—*

My heart turned to wood.

    *I am sorry Meed   Asa is dead   I know how you loved that
ox   I am sorry*

A wood heart will pump wood blood and soon enough you are wood all over.

I did not wish to breakfast with Asa's killer. But I had a wood tongue and could not speak.

After a long silence I said it were *cruel of Tom to lie so*   As far as Big known, Tom had only played a vicious trick on him.

Big said *Tom has good as murdered Asa*

Even with wood brains, I known that evil luck had killed Asa and that Big and Tom were innocent. But I still felt enough contempt to drown them both – with a ladle left over for myself.

I only said *Asa will have a coffin*

Big agreed it were right and fitting.

I were not sure how to tailor a coffin that size.

We sat in grief for Asa even as the idlers and loafers arrived to drink the day away. Big stayed and stared at the wall – at a bill posted amid Dog's library of rusted swords.

Steam Line on the Lakes,		
Comprising the following Boats:		
ROBERT FULTON,	CHARLES TOWNSEND,	NEW YORK,
DE WIT CLINTON,	PENNSYLVANIA,	UNITED STATES
	SHELDON THOMPSON	

> One Steam Freight Boat will leave Buffalo every day for Detroit and the intermediate Ports.
>
> One Steam Freight Boat will leave Buffalo every 10 days for Chicago and intermediate Ports.

After some time I realized that Big were waiting for Tom.

In general Tom Tod were not innocent of much. But he were innocent on the matter of Cloe's untruth. It is not always our sins we catch hell for. At the bee Tom had truly meant to congratulate Big. So it came as a great surprise when – before Tom could say hidy – Big grabbed him by the shirt and pinned him to Dog's rusty wall.

Are you pleased with your comedy?

Tom squirmed a great deal but did not lose his style.   *Hello Big I hardly noticed you*

You sent me to Cloe to make an ass out of myself

You were an ass already   but   I do not question her choice of bridegroom

She does not mean to marry me

Tom were stumped some and writhed at the old weapons poking his back.   *I will not call a woman a liar*

For a spell they only breathed at each other. If Big had let go of Tom, the eyeballs of every creature in the grocery would have held him in place. Even the stove fires seemed to stare at the two rivals, who were briefly beyond the use of language.

Big spoke first, through clenched teeth. *I will set you down from here   You will gather all your dandy s___   and board the next Buffalo boat   Choose east or west   Only that you stay gone from Ohio*

Or what?

Or I will remove your white teeth through your asshole

Tom smiled, like he were embarrassed by his own handsome teeth. *If it were another man's ass I would pay to see it   But I must decline your invitation   Out of a love of liberty*

We must rastle then   And the whipped one will leave

It is no match between us   It is not sporting   We ought to have a race instead

I swear I heard noses sniff around the room, tickled by the prospect of spectacle.

Big went right along, still snorting and snarling. *However you like I will beat you*

Tom did not have a ready answer. He swung his eyes around looking for one – until he seen the notice for *Steam Line on the Lakes.*

Boats   We will race boats   We will race steamboats

I haven't got a steamboat and neither have you

We are both men of means

Big wrung his lips some   *You can have a steamboat   I will swim and beat you   and after you can keep on your boat and   f___ off   to wherever you like   Anywhere but here*

Tom jumped to agree to Big's stakes.   *And if you lose you will do the same*

The whole assembly of drunks and cats and stoves was

holding their breath, and at that moment Dog's voice come up from the cellar. *If either of you had a* private appendage *half as long as your f___ing tongue you would make a man's wager   The loser roasted and eaten by the champion*

The talk were so wild that no one minded the speaker's being dead. Until Barse asked if that weren't Dog talking from the world beyond.

No   it were me   I said.   *You heard me*

Barse puzzled for a moment.   *That ain't legal Meed   A derby can't have murder in it*

Winter again.

To tell the story of Miss Sarabeth Strang you have got to know the story of Alonzo and Mary Bribb. If in that story you said Mr Alonzo sharpened his tongue with a strop, no one would debate you. If you went on to say that his Mrs Mary drank lye just to spit it at Mr Alonzo, no one would dissent. The Bribbs was the meanest two people in the history of Ohio, and it only made sense that they was married to each other. No one else could stand them.

So you could not fault Miss Sarabeth Strang for being shy of marriage. She were the Bribbs' domestic helpmeet and had seen their misery at close examination. Perhaps she considered that matrimony were the cause of their misery – and that to marry would make a Bribb of a person. But Sarabeth did not run off when Mr Burge Ramsey asked her hand. She only curtsied and gave a murmur no one knew for yes or no. Sarabeth generally kept quiet – not even a humming of hymns as she stitched or swept. It were figured that murmur meant she were amenable to Burge's offer, and Sarabeth did not indicate to the contrary. Burge Ramsey were not handsome or rich or clever or particularly reliable, but he were Christian and sober.

But no one can tell you any how their married life gone because on the night before the wedding supper Miss Sarabeth Strang turned to air. On the morning she was to wed, her mattress were empty as the grave.

Just like Carl Swarthout and Hiram Spurgeon, you would have to hunt down Sarabeth Strang to know the truth. But the general belief is that freedom spoke to her louder than comfort – she rathered to escape marriage altogether than to risk becoming a Bribb. In honor of her choice, we made a Webster's word of her name – to STRANG were to cut your own road through life's woods.

Our Cloe had run off a dozen times or more – to every corner of the state and places not on maps – different skins and skies. But she would always come back and say what her odyssey meant, what she seen, how folks done elsewhere. She always returned to tell us the story – shown us a handful of Ruth's barley from the fields of Judah.

On the day after the husking bee, Cloe Inches run off again. I would tell you a story on why she did it, if I had it to tell. But Cloe has got sole proprietorship of the matter. If you want to make a Webster's word of Cloe Inches, go find her yourself.

A contention. The national character favors MOTION above nearly everything else.

We have only put eagles and Geo Washington everywhere because you cannot draw MOTION. We are drunk for MOTION – to brag *six days to Louisville* and *a day to Detroit* and *direct from Newyork et c* To move, toward every compass point, always.

A second contention regarding CHANCE. If a matter exists, we will make bets on it.

The principal bet is business – sell a notion for more than you bought it. Prime lots or horseflesh. Speculations and expectations et c. But there are a thousand breeds of CHANCE. We bet on vegetable growing – chopping wood – all different types of rastling – climbing – marbles – foot races – horse races – roach races. Races put MOTION and CHANCE in angel harmony. Steamboat races are best of all.

We are guilty of nothing but our nature. They cannot hang us for that. There is not enough rope.

From the moment I met Tom Tod he were forever pulling notions from his pockets. Hard and soft money, watches, perfume water, marbles, penknives, silk kerchiefs, lucifer sticks. On the third day of December he topped himself and found a steamboat, bought from Buffalo sailors too skinned to pay for repair. His *Radish* were aged and somewhat on the runt side, but with a week of work from hired hands she were miles more boat than Big had.

A committee of competition – the grocery drunks and Mayor Frawley – convened and chose the lazy turnings of the river for a race way. The curves would even the odds between a steam engine and a man, and most important, folks along the banks could have a close view of the hilarity. From the northmost slip at Main-street around the first bend – past Big's ruined bridge at Centre-street – around Irish town bend and concluding at Mr Clark's bridge – a distance of one mile. Tom and Big agreed cheerfully and set the racing for a week before the New Year's wedding – so that the loser would never spend a second of 1838 in the new city.

That meant three weeks' more jawing. Not a word wasted on another topic – Big vs. Tom held the entirety of public interest. Not even the merger of cities were enough to turn heads.

Some folks held that Big would freeze in the December water and sink before fifty feet.
" " " " Tom did not know how to work his engine.
" " " " a mysterious third racer would arrive – revealed as Cloe herself.

THE RACE COURSE

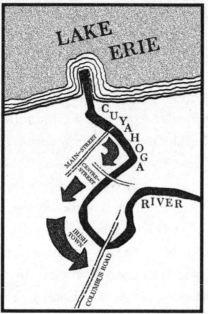

"   "   "   "   you should never bet against the
                              spirit of the times.
"   "   "   "   steam was the real spirit of the
                              times.
"   "   "   "   Tom's money were the real spirit
                              of the times.

I did not know what I held.

December in Ohio is not a handsome month. But on Saturday the twenty-third the sun and sky done their best to dress for promenade. The clouds arranged into a gingham, and the starved winter light had a smile to it. Cold air danced down from the north like even it wished to see the race, and the water frilled and twinkled in the breeze.

Old Dolores were dragged out and her nose tickled again. Her *krTTHWANNFFNG* sounded hoarse – wearied by so much celebration. People draped themselves in blankets and whiskey against the chill and collected at the river's edges. Tom could not help but make a festivity, and invited Frawley and the committee of competition aboard the *Radish* for merriment. He even had a militia band tooting bravely, shivering in their soldier suits. He brung on whiskey and cider and dandelion wine to grease the day. Between folks and musicians and refreshment, there were two tons of merriment aboard the *Radish*. At the center of this congress of turkeys were Tom himself, arrayed in a suit of screaming green – like he had stolen up every leaf of summer in his fabric. He slapped shoulders and laughed too hard and made bets on himself, acting nothing like a man at risk of banishment.

Ashore, Big stood apart from turkeys and all other creatures. His toes was lined up neat with the edge of the water, and his eyes watched nothing in particular. Whatever fury had driven him to the bet seemed gone, as were his fair-weather friends. There were ailing Mr Job wrapped in blankets – Mrs Tab at his side like she were holding him up – the seven Stileses – Philo – Oze – Dennes – no Cloe – no Asa. I stood a ways removed, not wishing to agitate Mr Job.

I considered if losing would cure my brother – set him free – set me free.

Everyone else mostly considered wagering. The public preferred Tom heavy, but there were always sports who would make odds.

The anxious merriment stumbled along until the noon hour, when cider-blushed Frawley waddled to the bows of the *Radish* and drew air into his bellows.

Ladies and gentlemen   Affairs of honor is illegal in this state   He struggled to extract an ancient pistol from his trouserfront.   *So I do not offer any official words*—with an unsteady hand he waved the gun high—*other than God bless this country and make it prosperous*

Fpprochk the pistol said by way of amen.

Straightaway Big stripped down to just his kerchief, setting his folded britches on a stone. He walked into the water until the river reached his chin, and took up long loping slaps.

Plisshf   plisshf   plisshf

Leisurely, Tom undid the ropes holding the *Radish* in

place and ambled forward to his boiler. Passenger Frawley went to pull in the gangway – but not before I scampered aboard. I had not planned to. Only the idea of a closer view grabbed me.

Tom Tod had taken it on himself to run the great stove that made the *Radish* go. Out of arrogance or sporting humor, he had not bothered to learn how to drive a boat in advance. It would not matter much. A steamboat gone at a blistering eight miles each hour, and even a fast swimmer could make barely two miles in that time. Tom would win without sweating.

The passengers took up parlor singing to pass the time—

Oh I don't want none of your weevily wheat
And I don't want none of your barley
But I want some flour and half an hour
To bake a cake for Charley

I went to the bow and watched my brother.

He were steady *plisshf*ing across water toward the first bend. A flotilla of ducks parted for him to pass through. Aboard the *Radish*, the singing kept up even as Tom clanked and cussed the engine. The crowds along the banks stretched out, as some folks ambled along to stay near Big and others stuck at the slip. Among them I could hear preachers and peddlers and cheerful Dr Strickland halooing about their various merchandise – Christ and fruit and kreosote.

* * *

Just as Big disappeared around the first bend, Tom hollered a triumph—

I HAVE GOT THE F___ER

The boat's great Ben Franklin stove coughed and cursed back – her pistons shrieked with delight – the *Radish* lurched. Drunken stumbles at first, but soon enough her paddlefeet rolled along at a slow stroll. The parlor singers were up to the part about *Charley is a dandy, the very lad who stole the striped candy*—but broke into whoops of delight at the feeblest MOTION.

The crowds on each side gone with us – trotting a ways and then stopping when they had got ahead – sitting on stones and fence posts to wait for us.

The *Radish* made no faster than a waltz for a quarter hour, and Big kept his lead. Fleet-footed Jonah Stiles dispatched himself to run back and forth between Big and boat to holler the progress of the derby.

Big is past the broken bridge

Tom laughed an itching way.

Off ran Jonah down the river path. If the boat were gaining speed I could only tell from the folks on the banks walking a bit faster.

Mayor Frawley and his friends took up the singing again.

Grab her by the lily-white hand
And lead her like a pigeon
Make her dance the weevily—

251

Tom said to *stop singing or I will put you in the boiler fattest first*

A few minutes more brought Jonah back – red cheeks panting.

Big is around Irish town bend

Big were close to three-quarters finished. Somehow he were on the cusp of winning – in truth Tom's lead-assed boat was on the cusp of losing more than Big were winning – but winning is winning, no matter how you fall to it.

At Jonah's latest report, Tom stood up from nursemaiding the boiler and gone to the refreshments. I expected he would have a drink to starch himself. But instead he went hunting among the barrels and bottles until he found a cask – which he grabbed up entirely. I seen as he took his drink back to the boiler that it had RELY ON STRICKLAND painted on the side.

Tom set the cask down and went into his pockets for his pearl-handled knife. With grand gestures he unfolded the tiny blade – raised it high – stabbed in the bung. He closed the knife gravely – lifted the cask to the boiler's door like it were taking communion – fed the boat a drink – strolled serenely to the bows – tugged at his green coat front.

Giving the boat a sip for courage eh Tom? said the puzzled mayor.

It is not whiskey   It is the dentist's kreosote

Frawley nodded sagely – as if it were common wisdom to feed steamboats so.

But I saw Tom's trick – nothing burned hotter than kreo-

252

sote. A boiler fire spiced with the substance would make a thunderstorm of steam.

Right away an awful hissing rose from the boiler – and not a minute later, the *Radish* shook with dispatch. The spectators on both sides gone from ambling to a brisk walk to a gallop to keep up. As we tore past Centre-street and the ruins of Big's bridge, only spryer legs could keep up. By the approach to Irish town bend it were only children and four-legged dogs. Our outrageous progress were not enough to please Tom. With each passing minute he splashed more and more kreosote into the boiler's burning gut.

The hissing went up to a roar – the iron skin of the boiler were blushing red with appetite. The *Radish* were hardly in the water at all but atop it. Tom grabbed up Frawley to help him work the ship's wheel as we roared around the bend. As we swung out wide, I could see Big and his small splashes a hundred yards ahead. Not another hundred yards past him were Mr Clark's bridge and the victory barrel bobbing beneath.

Tom looked at Big and back to his boiler – it would be close – close would not do – you cannot put "close" into a pocket for keeping. So he strolled back to the boiler – stooped – threw the entire cask of kreosote into the rabid flames. If the flames had teeth, they would have shone brighter than the sun.

I supposed there were tidiness in this outcome. Ohio city would be no more in a week's time, and Big Son – her resident spirit and architect – would head elsewhere. I confess I had been waiting for another of Big's miracles – for him to ride on the back of five hundred fish – or to run atop the water like a restless Christ. But instead he would make a brave effort but lose out to a dandy and his dentist medicine. Perhaps Big could keep swimming south, to the canal, to the Ohio, to the Mississippi, to New Orleans and the ocean beyond. His spirit had been born in a race and now it would extinguish in a race. Those were my considerations as Tom's *Radish* left Big in her wake. I do not know if he saw me aboard as he *plisshf*ed.

Tom gave an eagle cry and grabbed a pole to lance the victory barrel – but froze when he heard a sound like a bullet chewing the air.

Spkeeeew   and another   *spkeeeew*

The boiler were undoing her buttons.   *Spkeeeew*

Kreosote fire cannot be banked like wood fire.

Spkeeeewspkeeeewspkeeeew

I ran back from the bows – past Tom – past Frawley and the turkeys – past the boiler – as far from the fire as I could get – back toward Big. Before I reached the stern rail, something brighter than the sky swallowed me up.

Our trouble often travels by barrel – whiskey – apples – gunmeal – Tom's kreosote. When the last barrel burst, it loosed a whole summer of heat and blew the *Radish* to toothpicks. I learned how it was to be a bird without wings or feathers. The combustion sent me hurtling overboard, away from the bridge, back to Big and far past. As I gone overhead we swapped a glance for just a quick moment – swimming-Big and flying-Meed – the strangest hidy. I birded all the way back to the Irish town bend, where I caught in the winter bones of a tree. My landing scratched some, but it did give a fine view on the disaster.

You would never know the *Radish* had ever existed, but the fire from her boiler still burned. The explosion had sent a fine rain of liquid kreosote into the air. As the mist settled, the bits and bobs of flaming wreckage caught it to burning, and structures on both sides of the river followed the dance. The conflagration went faster than either racer, although Big did not stop swimming – only pounded the water faster and faster *plisshfplisshfplisshfplisshfplisshf* until he embraced the victory barrel.

From my distant tree I could not spy what face Big made when he finally seen the catastrophe. Underneath the bridge he had shelter from the fiery rain, even as the kreosote settled on the water, and the Cuyahoga itself burned around him.

Big did not pant for air or pout at the lack of celebration – he were happy to see his old foe flame back for a home-coming rastle. Straightaway he climbed up a great stone leg of Mr Clark's bridge and roared for *BUCKETS*. The burn-ing air warmed him right up, and he went for heroics like I had never seen. Once pails was circulating, he made himself into a rainstorm. He raced up and down the banks of the river stomping and smothering and dousing. He grabbed up folks out of burnings-up and set them a safe distance away. The redeemed, hairs singed and eyes wide, watched his naked person run and run and run – spreading like his own fire.

Even from my tree I could see his smile.

The kreosote fires ate up a half dozen houses on the Cleve-land side. On the Ohio side two entire streets were inciner-ated, plus a brick block of shops and factories. Included in the loss was the *ARGUS* printers and a thousand shinplasters and the plates of Big's own almanac.

The fire touched more than buildings – suitclothes and skin and civic spirit burned. The sky itself stayed draped in drab, and the river clouded over with ash. Somehow the bridge survived, only scorched, even though the *Radish* had bust so close by. Perhaps Dog's bombings had inoculated the bridge from exploding.

Not one bit of Tom Tod were turned up. Not any of the contents of his cavern pockets. Not any uncommonly white teeth.

Mayor Frawley landed a quarter mile beyond the explosion and did not survive his injuries. This only suited – Ohio city would not want any mayoring after the New Year.

Even though his body never showed, Tom Tod had himself a slapping good funeral. In truth a mess is the best burying stone. You cannot name a person who died and left every last speck cleaned up – you would not remember them from boredom. Keep your desolate places and Pyramids of Cheops. Exploding makes a better memory.

I do not know that my brother wanted any gratitude for fighting the kreosote fires. Wanted or no, there was no thanks offered. All those scorched eyes saw him like a wound that wanted washing.

Big Son ought to be in chains

Big Son ought to hang

I expect it was proposed that his liver ought to be pecked by eagles for misuse of fire. Eagles was deficient but the pecking could be done just as good by chickens.

It does not seem fair to blame Big entirely for the fire. He had not driven Tom Tod to use the kreosote. But he had been a party to the race, and without the race there would have been no fire. Since Tom were vanished to ashes, all the fault passed to Big like an inheritance.

It is resolved that you should depart from and never return to the cities of Cleveland or Ohio after the 1st of January 1838

The book of John does not tell how Lazarus of Bethany done before he took sick, or how he got on after his brief death. Whether the brother of Mary and Martha were the same type of man after resurrecting. Whether he sinned more or less or about the same amount. John only says that after Lazarus got over dying, they all had a banquet, and sister Mary poured perfume on Jesus.

I consider that Lazarus were already and forever dead in the breathing sense, and Jesus brung him back only to eternal life – to remembrance. Mr August Dogstadter were already dead when I pulled him from the river. When he came back alive in me, he were set on his usual behavior.

On Sunday the thirty-first of December 1837, I broke the Lord's sabbath and undertook to violate four other commandments and the laws of the state of Ohio besides. I rigged up ten trick barrels – split in two by hidden partition. I put whiskey into one side and Dog's gunmeal into the other. I done this ten times over, and then loaded the barrels in a wagon hired from Mr Ozias Basket.

I drove the wagon from my grocery at Pearl-street down the Columbus road hill, to the western landing of Mr Clark's bridge. I told the voice in the toll cabinet that I were delivering refreshments for the next day's grand ceremony of union. I said I would cross back directly and should not have to pay the toll. The voice in the cabinet disagreed. I did not bother to argue.

On account of it being Sunday the grocery were closed. A shame considering it were a prime occasion for refreshment – the last day of the year and the last day of Ohio city.

As 1837 went out, pots and pans were banged some – prayers spoke for a prosperous year. Once the streets gone silent and cold I stepped out – left dead Dog behind – and made a homecoming visit. I had a notion to put in my brother's mind.

The year 1838 had no moon or clouds yet, only stars blinking dumb as animals. No candles in the homeplace, no Asa in his stall. The only noise in the attic were Big's snores.

I knelt down and pinched his nose.

His breath moved to his mouth instead.

I kept his nose shuttered and put a hand over his trap.

With his breath dammed up, his eyes burst open.

I took away my hands.

Hidy Big

Little brother   I dreamt I were drowning   you should not be here

I will not be long   There is to be another bombing of the bridge   Dog lives and he is fixed on blood   There is powder hidden in the whiskey that I delivered for the festivities   and Dog means to explode it for wedding bells

Big looked unsure that his dream had ceased.

You are in poor favor   You are banished   but if you bring word to the authorities   Warn folks   You will be redeemed   Only you must get there before the ceremony

Big nodded slow as ice melting.

The last time I had walked down to the Cuyahoga at dawn, I wore nothing but pig s___ and a troubled mind. I had coat and shoes this time, but the vexation were worse. I did not know what I meant to do when I reached the water. I could let Big claim this feat and its reward. I could climb into the river and drown. I could say the whiskey were spoiled and pour out the barrels. I could confess. I could say nothing and walk until I forgot myself entirely.

No one ever seen the tolltaker come or go. No one knew for certain if he were one man or a trick-talking bird or a woman or a ghost. Only that the voice would have five cents for each person, animal and conveyance.

I approached with my hands spread out empty.

Five cents

I do not wish to cross

F___ off then

I am here to stop bloodshed

Five cents drunk or sober

There is another bomb

The voice said nothing.

My brother means to explode this bridge today   He has planted the powder already   He will come here soon   You will want a crowd to stop him

Acknowledgments

Ben Adams, Katie Adams, Joel Brouwer (you were right about punctuation), Alexandra Cook, Peter Ginna, Sally Howe, Michael Martone (huzzah), Jeffrey Melton, Doug Merlino, Monarch, Eric Nusbaum, Clifford and Lisa Lee Peterson at Taleamor Park, Aja Pollock, David Roth (not the one from Van Halen or magic), Sarah Scarr, Sophie Strohmeier, Alexa Tullett, Adam Villacin, Kellie Wells, and everyone at Scribner

Abundant and eternal thanks to:
Jim Rutman
Kathy Belden
My family—Beattys, Turners, and McConnells
Susan Beatty
My dad
My mom
Anna (the real Cloe)

About the Author

Pete Beatty is a Cleveland-area native. He has taught at Kent State University and the University of Alabama and currently works at the University of Alabama Press. He lives with his wife in Tuscaloosa, Alabama. This is his first novel.